Miss You, Mina
SUMMER
APPLE
CANDY

candy apple books... just for you.
sweet. fresh. fun. take a bite!

The Accidental Cheerleader by Mimi McCoy

The Boy Next Door by Laura Dower

Miss Popularity by Francesco Sedita

How to Be a Girly Girl in Just Ten Days
by Lisa Papademetriou

Drama Queen by Lara Bergen

The Babysitting Wars by Mimi McCoy

Totally Crushed by Eliza Willard

I've Got a Secret by Lara Bergen

Callie for President by Robin Wasserman

Making Waves by Randi Reisfeld and H. B. Gilmour

The Sister Switch
by Jane B. Mason and Sarah Hines Stephens

Accidentally Fabulous by Lisa Papademetriou

Confessions of a Bitter Secret Santa by Lara Bergen

Accidentally Famous by Lisa Papademetriou

Star-Crossed by Mimi McCoy

Accidentally Fooled by Lisa Papademetriou

Miss Popularity Goes Camping by Francesco Sedita

Life, Starring Me! by Robin Wasserman

Juicy Gossip by Erin Downing

Accidentally Friends by Lisa Papademetriou

Snowfall Surprise
by Jane B. Mason and Sarah Hines Stephens

The Sweetheart Deal by Holly Kowitt

Rumor Has It by Jane B. Mason and Sarah Hines Stephens

Super Sweet 13 by Helen Perelman

Wish You Were Here, Liza by Robin Wasserman

See You Soon, Samantha by Lara Bergen

by Denene Millner

SCHOLASTIC INC.

New York Toronto London Auckland
Sydney Mexico City New Delhi Hong Kong

For my daughters, Mari and Lila
who have long been waiting for their mommy
to write a book they're allowed to read
and
For girls with big hearts, open minds, and the ability to embrace others just the way they are . . . Mina is for you.

ISBN 978-0-545-25106-8

12 11 10 9 8 7 6 5 4 3 2 1 10 11 12 13 14 15/0

Printed in the U.S.A. 40
First Scholastic Book Clubs printing, May 2010

Chapter One

The one thing you need to know about me, like, right now? I so super-heart New York City — and especially the Brooklyn Bridge.

My stomach did double somersaults as my dad pulled the car onto Park Row and we passed City Hall. And then, standing at attention, was a big ol' pile of concrete and steel, arms open wide, waiting to hug our car and carry us over the East River. There were a gazillion buildings around us, and each building had a bazillion more windows, all of them peering out over what has to be the prettiest bridge in the world.

"I bet you it's not as pretty as the Golden Gate Bridge," my little sister, Maia, taunted, settling back into the pink pillow she brought along for the long ride from Greenwood, New Jersey. "Or the London Bridge."

"Whatever, Maia," I said, turning to look out the back window of the car.

I've never seen the Golden Gate Bridge in San Francisco, and I've only seen pictures of the London Bridge in one of Maia's picture books from when she was little. But how could those views even begin to hold a candle to what you see when you cross the Brooklyn Bridge? Unfolding right in front of my eyes was the Manhattan skyline — an amazing collection of buildings stretching up, up, up into the air, tossing glittery silver kisses into the sky. What's not to love?

"I like the George Washington Bridge better, anyway," Maia said, folding her arms. "You can see New Jersey from there."

"But you can't see the Statue of Liberty from the George Washington Bridge," I said, pressing my forehead to my window. "Dad, can't you get into the right lane?" I begged. "We get a better view from there."

My father waited for two cars to speed past us before he steered to the right, and I caught sight of her. There she was — the Statue of Liberty, lording over the water, her hand in the air, striking a fierce pose. I whipped out my drawing pad and turned to a fresh page. This time, I decided to sketch her crown. I hadn't done that in a while, and my skills had improved from January, the last time I speed-sketched Lady Liberty while we were crossing the bridge. So I think this piece could rock. Maybe Auntie Jill would think it was good enough to show off at the SoHo Children's Art Program, the fancy art camp where she works and that I would be attending for six glorious weeks.

I couldn't wait. No sister. No 'rents. Just me, my art supplies, my favorite aunt in her super-fabulous brownstone in Fort Greene, Brooklyn, and an art program I've been sweating since my auntie Jill started working there three years ago.

The only downside? I was already missing my best friends, Samantha and Liza, who I hadn't seen for ten days, not since we had our "See Ya Soon" going-away party. It wasn't easy going cold turkey without the two girls I've spent practically every second of every day with since we met on the soccer field in the first grade. We go to the same school and our parents visit one another on the weekends and holidays, and the three of us usually spend the entire summer hanging out together. But this year, Liza's parents were taking a massive road trip to somewhere random, and Sam's parents were vacationing on a beach somewhere with another family. So let's just say our "See Ya Soon" celebration felt more like a "My Besties Are Going to Be Gone Forever" memorial service.

"How many times are you going to draw that thing?" Maia huffed. "It looks the same way she did the last hundred times you made drawings of it."

Of course, my sister didn't know what she was talking about. I mean, every time I look at Lady Liberty, I see something new — something more beautiful than the last. Always changing.

"What do you care?" I shot back. "Is there a law somewhere saying I can't draw the Statue of Liberty?"

"Okay, you two — just stop it already," my mom said from the passenger seat. "You guys have practically five more minutes with each other before we drop Mina off at Auntie Jill's for the summer. Surely, you can go without arguing for that long. We all should be enjoying these last moments with Mina before we leave."

"Exactly," I said, taking my eyes off the statue just long enough to wrinkle my nose at my little sister. She mimicked my face, but kept her mouth shut. Thank goodness.

I knew Maia was giving me a hard time because she was jealous. While I was going to summer with

Auntie Jill, she was going to be stuck at home, helping out at the Akwaaba by the Sea Bed & Breakfast, my mom's part-time summer job. Not that I'd be complaining about *that*. In summers past, we got to go with Mom maybe once or twice a week, and the beach is just a two-minute walk from the B&B. And once breakfast was served and the rooms were straightened up, my mom was usually happy to hang out on the beach with us while we dipped in and out of the water and played beach games with her boss's kids.

My favorite place *ever* is the beach; nothing makes me happier than riding a choice wave on my boogie board and feeling the hot sand beneath my feet. Well, nothing except my art. My mom says I was born with a pencil in one hand and a paintbrush in the other; I love to paint, draw, collage, and build things, and think nothing of spending an entire Saturday morning making my own paper from recycled scraps, or building a fancy dollhouse out of discarded cardboard and gadgets I find around the house.

One of these days, maybe I'll be just like my favorite artist, Romare Bearden. I've loved his art ever since Mom bought me a book of it for Christmas. Maybe my art will travel the world from museum to museum, and people will buy it and put it up on their walls and call me an artistic genius. *She's the new Bearden,* they'll say. *Except she's a girl and not from Harlem.*

Yeah.

"Well, here we are," my mother sighed as my dad pulled into a space just down the street from my aunt's brownstone. "The beginning of a summer without my baby. In Brooklyn," she added, looking up and down the street disapprovingly.

"Come on, Mom, Brooklyn is awesome," I said as I watched my dad grab my suitcase. When he slammed the trunk closed, I practically sprinted down the block toward my aunt's brownstone. "My summer is going to be insane!"

"Uh-huh, that's my worry," my mom said as she headed up the staircase just behind my dad. He barely pushed the buzzer before my auntie Jill snatched open her carved mahogany door.

"Hey! You're here!" she said, pulling me into her embrace. "I'm so happy to see you!"

"Me too, Auntie Jill," I said, hugging her back. She smelled like warm vanilla and cinnamon; her lip gloss felt sticky on my cheek.

"Hey, hey — save some for me," my dad joked as he set my suitcase in the foyer. He gave his sister a kiss on the cheek. "Well, Jill, here she is, in the flesh — your little mini-me."

"You sure you're ready to play mommy for six weeks?" my mom asked Auntie Jill as she kissed her hello, too. "She thinks she's grown, but she's still new to the double digits. Twelve-year-olds can be a handful, you know."

"Mom!" I said, sucking my teeth.

"Well, hello to you, too, Miss April," Auntie Jill said to my mom, laughing. "Just for the record: I may be younger than you, but I think I can handle a twelve-year-old."

"See? There you go pointing out my age!" my mom laughed easily as Auntie Jill closed the door behind us.

"Aw, come on in here," Auntie Jill said. "Let me take a look at you. I feel like I haven't seen you all in ages."

"Since New Year's . . ." my dad chimed in.

"That's a shame, too," Auntie Jill said, cutting him off. "Y'all live in New Jersey, not Russia. It's only a few hours' drive to get here, you know."

"Well, you know how it is," my mom said. "Life gets in the way and we get busy, and sometimes two hours feels like twenty with these two fussing in the backseat of the car."

"Speaking of 'these two,' where's my Maia?" Auntie Jill said, peeking behind my dad's large frame. Maia was fiddling by the door, checking out the family photos on the parlor table by the door. "You better come give me some sugar!"

"Hi, Auntie Jill," Maia said, exchanging hugs and kisses with our favorite aunt.

"Aw, why the sad face, pumpkin?" Auntie Jill asked.

"Somebody thinks it would be way cooler to hang with her aunt Jill in Brooklyn than on the beach with her mother," my dad chimed in.

Frankly, I couldn't blame Maia. Auntie Jill is the fire. She's twenty-eight and lives alone in Fort Greene, Brooklyn, a fantastic neighborhood. She teaches art at a middle school right around the corner from her place; just down the street is the park, where she goes to play tennis with her super-hip friends; and the subway at the corner can take her anywhere she wants to go in New York City — all the museums, Rockefeller Center, Times Square.

I've been to her place only a few times — mostly, she drives out to see us during holidays because all of the family get-togethers happen at our house in Greenwood. But I get really excited whenever my parents announce a trip to Auntie Jill's house because I know she's going to have something incredible planned. Her friends, like her, are all funky artists who seem to spend their days painting and writing and singing and dancing and debating about politics and history and theory. Half the time, I don't know what the heck they're talking about, but I love to be a fly on the wall when they're laughing and arguing and performing — especially when Auntie Jill pulls out her easel and creates while her friends are singing or doing poetry or busting a move. I sit mesmerized, watching her toss back her locs while her pastels and her paintbrushes glide across the canvas.

Do you see what kind of summer I was about to have?

Now I just needed my parents to leave already, so that I could get the party started.

"Well, let me show you where to put your things, pumpkin. I set it up really nice for you," Auntie Jill said, taking me by the hand. When we all got to the top of the stairs, Auntie dramatically opened the door to her studio.

"This is it," she said, spreading her arms wide.

It was so beautiful, I had to catch my breath. The huge window was framed by sheer, floor-sweeping lavender curtains tied back with a sparkly silver string of oversize beads — the perfect complement to the soft sage green walls. A floor-length mirror graced the wall across from a daybed, which was piled deep with purple satin pillows — my favorite color. The opposite wall had a huge black square in the middle of it, with a basketful of pastels sitting on a shelf just to the right. Auntie Jill picked up a hot-pink chalk and scribbled *Welcome* across the wall.

"Lord, are we writing on walls now?" my mother asked, shocked.

Auntie Jill cracked up. "It's a chalkboard," she said. "See? It erases. It's a special kind of paint that you can use to turn the whole wall into one big canvas. I put it there so that Mina can draw and write little messages whenever she's inspired, and change them whenever she's tired of it. I'll take pictures of the really good ones before you erase them so you'll have a collection of your work to remember, okay?"

"But, Auntie, this is your studio — I can't sleep here," I said, taking a running leap onto the daybed. I didn't really mean what I said; I could sleep in that room forever.

"Oh, don't worry — this is still my studio," she said, pointing at her easel. On it was a palette of different shades of blue, and a canvas with a dibble of a few of the colors on it. Next to her easel was another — this one with my full name, Wilhelmina, written in script in purple marker across the bottom. "We're just going to share the studio while you're here — how about that?"

"Oh my gosh, is that easel mine?" I said, rushing over to the beige stand and gently running my fingers over it.

"Besides my great-grandmother, you're the only Wilhelmina I know," Auntie Jill laughed. "So that easel must be yours. Every real artist has one."

"Omigod, thank you, Auntie Jill," I squealed as I hugged her tight.

"Auntie Jill, when I get old enough to go to the art camp can I stay in your studio, too?" Maia asked.

"Eh — there's only room for one in this bed," I said quickly. I didn't want my little sister getting any ideas — she doesn't even like drawing or the color purple.

"Now, now — there's plenty of room up here for my little sweet potato," Auntie Jill countered. "Of course you can stay with me."

"But not right now!" I said, standing up and walking toward the door.

"Okay, then," my mom said. "I'm just going to go on ahead and assume that you still love me, even though you're rushing me out like you don't want your mommy around anymore."

"Love you, Mom," I said, extending my arms for an embrace. She kissed me on each cheek and then beckoned Maia over to the doorway.

"We'll call you when we get back home," my dad said to Auntie Jill while he hugged me tight. "And you, young lady: Behave, okay? Listen to your aunt Jill and help her out. Play this right and we just might let you come back next year."

"Come on, Dad, you know I'm the well-behaved one!" I laughed.

"Whatever," Maia said, clearly insulted by the joke.

"Uh-huh," Dad said.

My mother took my chin into her hands and ran her fingers over my chin-length reddish brown locs. "I love you — be good."

"I will — promise," I said, this time, fighting back tears as I gazed into her eyes.

"Okay, y'all — let's go," Dad said, heading down the stairs.

"Let me walk you out," Auntie Jill said, close on their heels.

My folks were barely down the bottom of the first landing of stairs before I was back on the day-bed, bouncing around and screaming in the pillows. I was so totally geeked about my new room and my new art space and my new camp! The only thing that would make it better was if Liza and Sam were there to enjoy my cool, posh new life. I made a mental note to send each of them an e-mail once I got settled and Auntie Jill showed me how to log on to her Mac.

I got up to grab my knapsack off the hallway floor where I'd dropped it; I yanked open the zipper and gingerly pulled out the framed picture of me, Liza, and Sam, hugging one another and grinning. We took that picture the day after school let out for the year, just as we were preparing for our big vacations away from one another. Sam's mom, who took the picture and framed a copy for each of us, had said, *So that you can take your best friends on your journey with you.* I'd been at my auntie Jill's for only about fifteen minutes, and already I had about an hour's worth of stuff to tell them.

I kissed the face of the picture of me and my best friends, and set it gingerly on the side table next to the daybed, and then headed back to the window to take in the view. It was Saturday afternoon and the block was filled with excitement — across the street and about eight brownstones down, a bunch of little girls were playing hopscotch and Double Dutch while their moms sat on the stoop talking; another few houses down on Auntie Jill's side, a few teenage guys were standing under a massive tree growing out of a small sidewalk garden, laughing and roughing one another up. A few people were headed to the corner bodega; others were headed to Fort Greene Park. Seeing all those people in little pockets up and down the street was a little intimidating; I didn't know how to Double Dutch, those boys were playing a little too rough for my taste, and though the park was just down the block, it looked like a whole new world, what with those tall buildings stretched out above the trees. As grown-up as I wanted my mom and dad to think I was, I was a little nervous about being out there in that big city by myself. I was going to need to lean on Auntie Jill for a little bit until I got more comfortable.

From my new bedroom window, I watched Auntie Jill hug my dad and mom good-bye, kiss Maia, and wave after the car as it pulled off down South Elliott Place, toward Lafayette Avenue. My head got a little hot and a couple of tears rushed to the corners of my eyes as I saw the car turn left and disappear down the road.

Moments later, Auntie Jill called up the stairs. "Mina? Baby, come downstairs, let me get a look at you." I wiped the tears from my eyes and checked my face in the mirror, then rushed down the stairs.

"So, buttercup, you hungry? I was in Manhattan last night and stopped by Zabar's to pick up some hummus and pita bread, a few olives, a couple of bagels, and little whitefish, and some fresh strawberries for brunch."

Auntie Jill got the side-eye for that one. Love her to pieces, but, um, whitefish? Olives? *Hummus?* Maybe it was a mental block, I don't know, but I totally forgot that my auntie was a vegetarian. I'm talking tofu turkey for Thanksgiving. Trust me when I tell you, that didn't go over too well when my auntie brought her dish to our family holiday gathering last November. She got clowned like you wouldn't believe when she sat it next to the honey baked ham and asked my mom if she cooked the collards with meat. "It's Thanksgiving," Daddy had laughed. "You'll live if a little smoked pig finds its way to your stomach. You better act like we were raised in the same house, forks on pork!" The whole house rocked with laughter over that one; Auntie Jill took it in stride, but I can tell she gets a little wound up when people question why she thinks smashed chickpeas and hard, chewy, flat bread is the height of fine dining.

"Don't worry," Auntie Jill said, pulling me close and cracking up at the funny look on my face. "I'll eat the whitefish; you can have the bagels," she said. "I even bought cream cheese."

I gave her another look.

"No, it doesn't have scallions in it," she added, knowing instinctively that I was about to question which kind she'd purchased. The last time Auntie Jill served me a bagel with cream cheese, she spread the scallions on really thick. Let's just say it wasn't exactly a favorite.

"Tell you what: I'll go get our spread together and we can sit out on the stoop and catch up. Why don't you go back upstairs and finish putting away your things — I'll call you when everything is ready."

"Okay," I said, bounding up the stairs.

See? That's why I love me some Auntie Jill: She just gets me. Even though she wasn't going to be packing any ham sandwiches in my lunch for camp, she knew what I liked. Purple definitely tops the list. As does art. Math, too. Oh, and celebrity watching.

Who doesn't like to see famous people up

close? Not that I ever have. Well, I did see Al Roker, the weather guy from the *Today* show, once at the beach on the Jersey shore. He was staying at the Akwaaba B&B for vacation with his family. My mom wouldn't let me go say hi, though. Plus, Liza said he doesn't count as a celebrity because he's a weather guy — no different from Sam's dad, Mack Macintosh, who's the weatherman on the local cable station back in Greenwood. But Al Roker is on TV and anyone who's on TV is famous in my book — even Sam's dad. I didn't feel like arguing with Liza over it, though.

Anyway, my aunt was always telling me about the famous people who live and hang out and perform in Brooklyn. Maybe one of them would walk by while Auntie and I were sitting outside. I wondered if my celebrity crush, Corbin Bleu, ever visited Fort Greene. He lived in California, but Brooklyn would be a hip enough place for him to show his face, right? Maybe I'd see him here. Maybe I could get an autograph. Or a picture!

I reached into my book bag and pulled out the Kodak EasyShare digital camera my parents got me for Christmas and slipped the handle of the tiny camera bag over my wrist. Then I picked up a purple pastel, and wrote *Mina IS here!* in big bubble letters all the way across the chalkboard wall, and finished it with striped stars and polka-dot flowers.

I stood back and, arms folded, admired my work and smiled.

Yeah, this summer was going to be the best ever!

Chapter Two

There were a million people rushing down the street that first morning — so many it made me woozy.

There were moms with their kids, teenagers with their friends, and people with briefcases, some in suits, others dressed in casual summer gear — all of them moving like a wave headed toward the start of their day. I struggled to keep up with Auntie Jill, who was practically leaping down Fulton Street.

"Pick it up, Mina," she said easily while she breezed through the crowd headed toward the subway. I was way behind her, huffing like I was in the middle of a five-mile run. The new art-supplies box my mom gave me as a going-away present felt like I was carrying a plump ten-year-old down the street. "If we catch a number four train in the next few minutes, we just might make it to camp early enough for you to see the instructors' artwork in the teachers' gallery."

"Okay," I said simply, because that was about all I could manage as I chased her down the subway stairs and into the cavernous underground station. It was hot down there and it kinda smelled; I was convinced the place was a lab for germ nastiness on the level of the mold experiment we did in science class just before summer break. I made a mental note: *Don't touch anything in the subway.*

Auntie Jill took one look at my face, shook her head, and cracked up. "You'll get used to the subway quicker than you think," she laughed as if she could read my mind. She handed me a small yellow card, then headed for a turnstile leading onto the platform. "Keep your MetroCard in a safe place, okay? You're going to need it to get to all of the different places you and your class will be traveling for your art assignments."

I watched Auntie Jill swipe her card and push through the turnstile, and then I did the same, just as the train rushed into the station. We walked double time to the yellow line, my aunt holding on to my wrist as she squeezed past a couple of people. Standing to my right was a girl about my age, effortlessly hoisting an art-supplies box twice the size of mine to look at the oversize hot-pink watch on her left wrist. She caught me staring and smiled. I quickly turned my head toward the opening subway door and moved a little closer to my aunt, who was about to make her move onto the train.

There weren't any seats on the train and because my hands were full with my art supplies and I wasn't used to riding a subway, I forgot to brace myself for takeoff. And what do you know? As soon as the train pulled out of the station, I went flying into the girl with the hot-pink watch.

"Omigod, I'm so sorry," I told the girl, grappling for the silver pole and trying to catch my footing before I fell to the floor. I dropped my MetroCard at the feet of a man with sneakers the size of a small canoe. As I fumbled around on the floor trying to retrieve the card, I could feel practically every eye in the car trained on me. If I had the power to melt into a little puddle and drip out of the cracks of the heavy metal doors, I would have done it, for sure.

"Um, yeah. The poles are a perfect way to keep that from happening again," the girl said as she grabbed my elbow to help me up. She giggled, so

I guessed she hadn't meant it to be mean. I cringed. *Nice! As if I'm not already embarrassed enough,* I wanted to say. Instead, I mumbled, "Thanks."

"Here, let me take your art box, honey," Auntie Jill said. "You okay?"

"Uh, yeah, I'm okay," I said, running my fingers over my neon-green miniskirt, swiping at imaginary dirt and trying really hard not to look like a total dork in front of all of New York City.

"Nice art box," the girl said as she moved her hand on the pole to make room for mine. "I saw one just like it at Pearl when my mom took me to buy mine. You an artist?"

I hesitated. I didn't really know what to say back, or even if she expected me to speak to her. And what in the world was "Pearl"? I sure wasn't about to ask her, though, because the girl said it like I was supposed to already know. I settled on a weak "Kinda."

"Actually, my niece is quite talented and well on her way to becoming an artist," Auntie Jill chimed in. She clearly couldn't help herself from bragging about me. Embarrassed, I fought back a groan. "I see you have an art box, too — are you an artist?" she asked the girl.

"I want to be." The girl smiled warmly. "I'm

actually on my way to the SoHo Children's Art Program. Today's my first day."

"Really? What a coincidence! I'm an instructor there, and my niece Mina is going to be in the camp, too," Auntie Jill said excitedly. "What's your name?"

"Gabriella," she said, rolling the "r" in her name and giving a little wave.

"Well, it's nice to meet you, Gabriella. You look really familiar to me for some reason," Auntie said, tilting her head to the side. I took a closer look at the girl, too; she had an olive complexion and long, brown hair pulled into a curly mass at the top of her head.

"Aren't you one of the art teachers at Brooklyn Tech?" Gabriella asked.

"Yes — yes, I am," Auntie Jill said, squinting her eyes as if that was going to help her recognize the girl. "Forgive me, but you don't look old enough for Brooklyn Tech."

"No, no — I don't go to Tech. But my brother does. He's in the science program and takes some of the art classes. I think I've seen you at a few of the art shows there?"

"Oh! Who's your brother?" Auntie Jill asked, the excitement in her voice rising.

"Kent Diaz. He's in the eleventh grade."

"Oh! I know Kent! He wants to be an architect, right?"

"Right," Gabriella said, smiling.

"Small world," Auntie Jill said. "See, Mina?" she added, turning toward me. "You're not even at the camp yet and you've made a new friend."

I gripped the pole a little tighter and tossed a halfhearted grin in the girl's direction, then focused my attention on the *Sam* and *Liza* my girls had scribbled on my lucky purple Converse. I'd designed my sneakers on the Converse website all by myself. The funky green stripe up the heel and the starry lavender and neon-pink laces I found at Target made them look superspecial. I was wearing them when I got the A on my math final, and when I applied for the summer art camp, which had only fifteen openings, but from what Auntie Jill said, hundreds of applications, so it was safe for me to assume that my sneakers were lucky. Sam and Liza got ahold of them just before we all left for summer vacation and signed their names on the sides with special sparkly white marker, reminding me the entire time they were scribbling not to forget them while I was at my "fancy art camp."

But as for Gabriella? I wasn't sure if she'd be

real friend material. Suddenly, I missed Liza and Sam more than ever.

The subway conductor warbled some message over the loudspeaker and then the train screeched to a halt. This time, I held on tight to the pole until the doors opened at a station named City Hall. There, Auntie Jill, Gabriella, and I transferred to the number six train, and then got out for good at the Spring Street station.

With Auntie on my right and Gabriella on my left, we made our way up the concrete steps, headed out of the dungeon darkness up toward the light. As my foot hit the top step, a miracle unfolded before me: Manhattan at rush hour.

It was a complete attack of the senses — the smell of coffee competing with the fumes of the taxis that were darting up the streets at top speed and nearly scraping the curbs to pick up stylish passengers. It was so loud — so much noise! People yelling into their cell phones, feet stomping, horns blaring — everyone moving in this massive synchronized dance.

I looked for all the bright lights and neon signs and huge billboards that were in Times Square, but there were none here. Instead, there were vintage shops and art galleries and delis with a cornucopia of fruit in the window, and all these stylish stores. There were equally stylish people who stalked the sidewalks like top models on a runway, with their high-heeled shoes and their crisp jeans. There were people with tattoos and funky hair and leather jackets, even though it was already eighty degrees outside. If I weren't so fascinated by the sights, I might have been a little scared. But SoHo was beautiful, with its cobblestoned streets like a red carpet to the coolest, chicest neighborhood on the planet. Fort Greene, I decided right then, would be a fine place for my first apartment, but when I moved up and got rich and famous, I was going to come straight to SoHo. This place had Grown-up Mina written all over it. Well, except for the tattoos and spiky hair.

It wasn't Greenwood; that's for sure.

"Okay, everyone, come on in and put your art supplies next to an easel, then cop a squat here on the rug — we're going to go ahead and dive right in," Ms. Roberts said as she ushered us into the huge sixth-floor loft.

Fifteen easels stood at attention on the far end of the room, each facing ceiling-to-floor windows overlooking Broadway. A colorful, oversize rug spread lazily across the wooden floor.

I tried hard not to seem like I was all pressed about which easel I'd set my stuff next to. But I really wanted one in the middle — not in the front, because who needs all *that* attention, and not in the back because you can only see the buildings and the busy street below if you're peeking around somebody's canvas and head. Just as I figured out which easel I wanted and took two steps toward it, another girl ran-walked past me and plopped her oversize sky blue art tote right in front of it. Her tote said PAULETTE in bold, dark blue letters. She tossed me a half smile and an eye roll, and then beckoned another girl — a tall, thin, redhead whose name tag read MARISKA — over to the easel next to her.

I shifted awkwardly to avoid the stampede, and ended up standing in front of an easel in the back. All I could see was the back of Paulette's blond head. Gabriella sauntered up and dropped her art box at the foot of the easel to my right.

"Nice view, huh?" she whispered.

I shrugged. I missed Auntie Jill already. She was upstairs, teaching a class of sixteen-year-olds. Everyone in my classroom looked to be about my age.

"So, I'd like to go over with you all of the wonderful projects we'll be studying this camp session," Ms. Roberts began, beckoning us back over to the rug. "We've got some exciting things lined up and I just know you art lovers are going to have a fantastic time."

Paulette, trailed by Mariska and another girl named Stephanie, tumbled onto the rug, laughing easily and gabbing as if they didn't have a care in the world or any interest in what Ms. Roberts had to say.

"Okay, simmer down," she said as the last of us plopped down. Her assistant passed out sheets of paper to us students; our instructor waited until the room was absolutely quiet before she began again. "We have six weeks to complete four major pieces. The goal is for each of you to get some insight into the works of some great artists, and then we'll take you out all across this magnificent city to help you get inspired as you create your own masterpieces."

I looked down at the list and felt a rush of excitement. We were going to visit a bunch of places I'd seen only in movies, never in person. The Metropolitan Museum of Art. Rockefeller Center. The world-famous toy store FAO Schwarz. They'd mentioned in the camp brochure that we'd get to draw some of New York's most famous landmarks. But I hadn't expected that in a matter of a few weeks I'd be able to see all the places I'd spent a lifetime craving to visit. *Yes!* I wanted to shout out loud. But I knew better.

"We've seen some terrific work come out of this camp, and every year at the end of the session, we have a big art show featuring one piece each of you create based on what you've learned," our instructor continued. "Your pieces will be evaluated by an esteemed panel of local artists and art teachers who will help me decide which of all of the work created here during this session is worthy of being featured on the cover of the SoHo Children's Art Program's Fall catalog. That means that one of you will leave this summer's camp a published artist. How exciting is that?"

A buzz raced through the room.

"So, we're going to be spending a lot of time together traipsing all over Manhattan over the next few weeks. Why don't we get to know one another? I'd like each of you to introduce yourselves, tell me who your favorite artist is, and what kind of art you most enjoy creating. I'll start with myself: I'm Jada Roberts, a fine arts professor at New York University where I've been teaching for the past eight years. I'm the head instructor for the grades seven through nine group here at the SoHo Children's Art Program, where I've worked for three summers now. My favorite artist is Monet, and I'm sure you'll learn more about why as we complete our program. He is quite the inspiration. Now, who are you?" she asked, peering out over the rug at the sea of heads before her. Most everyone looked at one another, too afraid to be the first to speak up.

Except Paulette, who dove right in.

"Well, I'm Paulette, but you already knew that!" she said with a giggle.

"Absolutely! How could I forget the winning artist of last year's competition?" Ms. Roberts boomed. "Everybody, Paulette's piece was featured on the programs for this past school year. I had the distinct pleasure of seeing her watercolor of Rockefeller Center on literally thousands of magazines. Those magazines went out to NYU students all across the country. It was quite beautiful. So, Paulette, I know you're a huge Monet fan as well. Has that changed since last summer?"

"Oh, I'm still in love with Monet, but that's so last year for me. This year, I'm totally feeling Van Gogh. He's all dark and mysterious and unpredictable and this year is all about being original," Paulette insisted, slouching back and exchanging knowing glances with her friends, who looked like they had to practically sit on their hands to keep themselves from applauding. "And I've only gotten better since last year, so you're going to see even greater things from me this summer."

Wow. Well, she's not shy, huh? I thought to myself. *Or humble.*

"For those of you who don't know me," she added, "I'm in the eighth grade at Arts and Sciences School here in Manhattan, and this is my third year at Camp SoHo. And, oh yeah, I paint to win. Just so you know."

"Thank you, Paulette," Ms. Roberts said. "You'll be happy to know that you have some pretty stiff competition this year. We've got some strong new talent," she added, grabbing a piece of paper off the lectern and peering at it over her glasses. "Who is . . . Let's see . . . Wilhelmina Chestnut?"

Uh, am I having an out-of-body experience, or did the teacher just call my whole name out loud? I thought. The only person who ever does that is my mother, and that's only when she's mad and I'm in big trouble.

"Wilhelmina?"

"That's me," I squeaked. Literally squeaked. Totally embarrassing. I cleared my throat quickly, hoping nobody caught it, but judging by Paulette's smirk, I might as well have squeaked into a bullhorn.

This time, much louder, I said, "Everybody calls me Mina. That's my, um, nickname."

Paulette and her buddies giggled. I forced myself to keep facing forward, but I could feel my cheeks getting hot. I wished Ms. Roberts would go on ahead and say what she had to say and then call on someone else.

"Oh, okay, Mina," Ms. Roberts said. "Well, I'll tell you this much: I'm really excited to see your work. Your aunt tells me you're quite gifted."

"Yes, ma'am," I blurted because I really didn't know what else to say. Out of the corner of my eye, I saw Mariska mouth the word "ma'am," which earned a few more giggles from the girls surrounding her. All except for Paulette, who was busy picking imaginary lint from her T-shirt and acting like she couldn't hear a thing, though it was very clear she was clinging to the instructor's every word.

"Okay, everyone," Ms. Roberts said, "if you look on the back wall by the art supply area, you'll see some of your work on display. Mina's is the collage. It's quite colorful. Take a look when you get a chance. So tell me, Mina: Where are you from and who's your favorite artist?"

I adjusted the bandanna holding my locs back from my face. "Um, I'm from Greenwood, out in central New Jersey," I managed to get out, though I felt like my tongue was about five times its normal size. "This is my first time at art camp. My favorite artist?" I pushed out a little more confidently. "Definitely Romare Bearden."

"Romeo who?" Paulette asked, all loud. Of course, she got lots of snickers with that one.

"Romare Bearden," I heard a voice from behind me say, enunciating each syllable. I whipped around to see who had come to my defense. It was Gabriella. "He's a pretty awesome artist who specialized in collages. You should check him out sometime," she added. She looked at me and mouthed, "You're welcome."

I mouthed, "Thank you." Maybe Gabriella could be a friend after all.

"Well, I look forward to seeing more of your work, Mina," Ms. Roberts said, smiling. She looked back at her paper. "Now, who's next? We have a new camper from Connecticut . . . Lisa?"

After a half hour of more introductions, reading through the assignment sheet, and a lesson on paint mixing, Ms. Roberts let us break for lunch. I was grateful, because in addition to being tied in a thousand nerve knots, my stomach had started to growl loud enough to draw attention. Blame it on Auntie Jill, who thought it was a good idea to serve natural oatmeal with raisins for breakfast. I didn't have the heart to tell her I don't do oatmeal; I just pushed it around in my bowl enough to make it look like I was enjoying it. Really, what I'd wanted was some pancakes or sausage with eggs.

"Everybody's going to Lombardi's pizzeria just down the way," Gabriella said as I swirled my paintbrushes in a plastic container full of water in the sink. "Toby and I were going to walk over together. Want to come?"

Just as Gabriella made her pitch, Paulette strutted over to the art supply area, a few girls in tow. "I mean, I looked at it when we came in, but I didn't see what the big deal was. And I still don't," she said, stopping right in front of the wall of student art. She didn't call out any particular piece, but she was staring right at my collage as she spoke. "I remember doing something like this," she said. And going for maximum dramatic effect, she added: "In my third grade art class!"

Her friends all laughed as if they were in an orchestra and she was their conductor.

Wow. Did she really just dis me like that in front of half the class? I wondered. Mortified, I bent over into the sink and and tried my best to look like I hadn't heard what she said.

"Anyway, come on, people!" Paulette continued, clapping her hands to call everyone's attention away from the wall. "Lombardi's awaits, and you know how grumpy I get if my special table isn't there. Let's move it out!"

Gabriella looked at Paulette over her shoulder and shook her head. "Good grief," she sighed, before turning back toward me. "Anyway, so you want to roll with us or what?"

"Sure. Why not?" I said. "What's that all about, anyway?" I added, nodding my head toward Paulette, who was heading for the door with at least five other girls following fast on her heels.

"Ugh, don't pay her any mind — save your brain cells for things that really matter," a tall, wiry, blond guy said as he walked up to us. He extended his hand. "Hi, I'm Toby Sheppard."

"Hey," I said, taking his hand into mine.

"Toby, Mina. Mina, Toby," Gabriella said. "I met Mina on the subway this morning."

"Nice to meet you," I said, trying to shift my focus from Paulette to the conversation at hand. "What's her deal, anyway?" I asked.

"Who, Paulette?" Gabriella asked. "Well, long story short, she's been here three summers in a row, and she's won the competition the last two years, and let's just say she's not lying when she says she paints to win."

"Yeah, she doesn't exactly play well with others," Toby added while he inspected my collage. "Hey, this is really nice. I love how you used watercolor and ripped paper to make the ocean. Is this your first time here?"

"Where, in Manhattan?" I asked, a little confused.

Toby laughed and looked at Gabriella, and she, in turn, looked at me, then cocked her head to the side. "Wait, *is* this your first time in Manhattan?"

"Well, not exactly," I said, feeling my cheeks get hot. "We've driven through it before on our way to my aunt's house."

I realized after I heard the words coming out of my mouth that what I just said was even worse than saying I'd never been to Manhattan before. Gabriella put me at ease, though.

"Hey, that's more than I can say for a few kids who live around my way — and we live in Brooklyn," Gabriella chimed in.

"Don't sweat it. My first time was last year, when I came to this camp. It's definitely a cool way to get to see the city," Toby added. "Anyway, you hungry?"

"I could eat," I said, smiling.

"Okay, well, let's do it, then," Toby said, rubbing his hands together. "Lombardi's is the perfect introduction to Manhattan. Let's be sure to get pepperoni on our pizza."

For the first time that entire day, I felt myself relax. Paulette made it crystal clear she didn't intend to play nice. But I was happy that Gabriella and Toby did.

"Sure," I said easily. And with that, the three of us headed out the door, down the elevator, and out into the bustling, energy-filled street, the warm sun lighting our way.

Chapter Three

I didn't want to come off like a total newbie in front of the entire class, but when we got to the corner of 82nd Street and Museum Mile, I practically melted into the sidewalk.

The Metropolitan Museum of Art was a big mass of awesome. I literally had to resist bolting up the steps that stretched up and into the museum. In fact, the only thing that kept me from doing that was all of the activity outside the museum: There were artists selling their sketches, vendors serving hot dogs, and people from all corners of the earth speaking different languages as they, too, took in the scene.

"Pretty cool, huh?" Gabriella said, clearly seeing the stars in my eyes.

"Yeah, it's nice," I said, trying to play down my excitement.

"Wait until you see what's inside," she said as we made it up the stairs. "I overheard Ms. Roberts saying that if we have time, we might get to see the Temple of Dendur. It's bananas!"

"*Please*," Paulette chimed as she walked lazily past Gabriella and me. "It's okay and all, but after you see it for, like, the billionth time, it's not all that deep. Now, the Frick museum? That's the place to be."

Gabriella looked at me and rolled her eyes. I looked straight ahead and kept my mouth closed. I'd promised myself I'd stay out of Paulette's mini-drama, and I meant to stick to that. Besides, I was too excited to get inside the Met. We didn't have anything like this back home, and after a while, you can only look at the County Historical Museum so many times before it's a total snore. I was hoping, too, that I'd be able to sneak around and learn a bit about Georgia O'Keeffe, Claude Monet, and some of the other artists Ms. Roberts had been talking about back in class earlier that morning.

"Okay, everyone, right this way," Ms. Roberts called out to the group as we made our way through the doors. "So, as I explained, we're here for a guided tour of the new Picasso exhibit, and we're going to check out a few of the museum's staples in the Impressionist wing. We'll also stop in to see the Temple of Dendur if we have time. But before we leave, I want you all to pick your favorite Picasso portrait, and then sketch it as if it's your own self-portrait. Time is limited, so let's hurry. Be sure to stick with me and the museum guides at all times, and when in doubt, look for the red camp T-shirts; this will help all of us get back to SoHo safely."

The grand hallway was like something out of a movie. We followed a businesslike museum guide up a sweeping flight of stairs into a quiet, large, looping hall where dozens of Picassos hung like bold splashes of color across the walls. A couple of us students — me included — squealed at the sight. Truth was, I'd never imagined that I'd see a Picasso up close.

"So, friends, you already know that Picasso was an incredible Spanish painter and sculptor who was one of the most prominent artists of the twentieth century . . ." the guide began.

"Oh, good grief — who wants to stand here and listen to a lecture? Blah blah blah — I want to see the paintings already," Paulette said not so quietly. She grabbed Mariska's hand and slunk off to the other side of the room, boldly walking past

Ms. Roberts. A few more of the campers followed behind them, leaving only a handful of us standing there, politely listening to the guide. She *was* boring. But really, was that any excuse to be rude?

"Well, it looks like we're losing a few of the class members," the guide said, after droning on for a little while longer. "How about we go ahead and take a look at some of the pieces and talk as we walk along? "

"Good idea," Gabriella whispered.

We inched along the walls, admiring a collection of paintings from Picasso's Blue Period, and through another room that showed a bunch of paintings that looked like they'd been painted, cut into tiny squares, and then glued back together again.

"These are my favorites!" Paulette announced loudly, bullying her way through a crowd of gray-haired ladies wearing identical blue shirts to stand directly in front of one of the larger paintings. Following her lead, the guide called all of us over.

"So, who can tell me what period these paintings fall into for Picasso? Anyone?" the guide asked. Her eyes pored over the sea of red T-shirts standing before her and landed on . . . me. "What's your name, young lady?"

I looked behind me. Nope, no one there. "Uh, me?" I asked, pointing at my own chest.

"Yes," she said. "Your name?"

I heard a few giggles to the left and right of me. "I'm Mina."

"Okay," she said. "Picasso was known for changing his style, and through the years he had several different periods of works. We just came out of the collection from his Blue Period, and we started with the Rose Period. Which is this?"

I froze. The guide stood there staring at me, like I was some Picasso expert who walked around spitting out Picasso facts. I had no clue what the answer was. Someone — I think maybe Paulette — started humming the theme to the game show *Jeopardy* — a ditty that made practically the entire room fall into hysterics. I think even one of the little old ladies was giggling.

"Um, the beige period?" I mumbled. Hey, a couple of the pictures had a lot of beige in them, and seeing as the other two periods were named after colors, I figured I'd give it a shot.

Paulette led the laugh parade. "Did she just say 'the beige period'?" she asked, clutching her stomach for added effect. "Wow. Just . . . wow."

Then she took two dramatic steps back from the display and jabbed her finger up toward the top of the wall. My eyes followed the tip of her finger to a sign that said in bright, bold red letters: PICASSO AND THE CUBIST MOVEMENT.

"It's called Cubism," Paulette snarled.

I felt my cheeks burn. *Embarrassing.*

"Yes, very good. It's called Cubism," the guide continued without missing a beat.

"Don't even sweat it," Toby whispered in my ear.

"For real," Gabriella whispered. "What counts is what you're going to do on your sketch pad. Did you see something you liked? I'm all over that one over there — the one where the lady has two eyes on the wrong side of her nose. I think I'll name it 'Paulette.'"

I was in no laughing mood. "Maybe I'll just stick to this one," I managed.

"Well, you know, if you're into it, make it happen," Gabriella said. "Easy breezy."

Determined to put Paulette out of my head, I flipped to a clean piece of paper in my sketch pad and reached into my purse for my pencil. Then I looked up at Picasso's painting again. It really was beautiful; it was a stack of squares in different sizes, arranged to look like a woman. Some of the squares were beige and different shades of brown; some were gray and some were even black, with a little green in them. The more I leaned into the picture and looked at the details more closely, the cooler it became. In fact, I thought it looked more like a collage.

Inspired again, I found a seat on a bench opposite the painting and stared at it some more. No, a pencil wasn't going to do. I needed glue. I tore into my purse and fumbled past my raspberry lemonade smoothie lip balm, a half-eaten pack of grape Now and Laters, a hair tie I use to keep my locs tied back while I paint, my wallet, and a pack of fine-tipped Sharpies (minus the forest green one, which I still think my little sister stole, seeing as it's her favorite color and it was the color of the word *Mommy* she'd written in bubble letters on the homemade birthday card she'd made for my mom. She's such a little thief!). Ah, there it was: a glue stick.

I reached into my jacket pocket and pulled out the map and flyers the guide gave us before we started our tour, and slowly started ripping them to pieces. Once I had a sufficient pile, I picked up my pencil, studied the painting again, and, in my mind, imagined the woman with chocolate brown skin and flowing locs, and a hot-pink dress instead of a beige one. Yeah, I could make her real cute, I decided.

Just as I picked up my pencil to draw the outlines of what would be my version of Picasso's painting, Paulette plopped down next to me on the bench. She, too, flipped to a clean page and then waved her pencil in the air like it was a wand and she was about to do a magic trick. I tried not to look in her direction, but she wasn't having it.

"Funny," she said, leaning close enough for me to smell the sour lemonade lip gloss she'd slathered on her lips after sketching a portrait across the hall. "I didn't think you'd pick this one, seeing as you didn't even know what it was."

My tongue was tied into too many knots to come up with a snappy comeback. So I just kept working, trying my best to act like I wasn't paying her any mind. But that just made her lean in closer.

Paulette looked around to see who was watching, and then she asked in a low voice, "No offense, but why are you here, anyway?"

I snuck a quick look at her and then buried my eyes back onto my sketch pad. "It's a camp trip," I mumbled. "The whole class is here."

"No, I mean why are you *here* — in New York, at this camp?" Paulette said, this time turning her body toward mine.

Silence.

"I mean, maybe it's just me, but you don't seem to really know all that much about art, so . . . it seems kinda weird that you're going to an art camp," Paulette continued as she scratched her pencil across her sketch pad.

More silence.

"Don't get me wrong: It's cute and all that you do the little glue-and-paper thing," she said, nodding her head toward me as I nervously glued a piece of torn museum map to the squares I'd drawn on the paper. "But really, outside of, like, a third grade art class, are we calling that art these days?"

This time, a lump in my throat, and the beginnings of tears.

Maybe she was right.

"I'm just saying . . ." Paulette was about to continue, but Ms. Roberts cut her off.

"Wow, look at you two!" she said, completely oblivious to the torture Paulette was laying on me. "This is pretty good stuff. See how art works? Here you are, Paulette, taking a classical approach, and Mina! You're taking it up a notch with the collage. You know, contemporary artists like Bearden studied Picasso and picked up a thing or two from his Cubist work. Very perceptive. But Mina, I don't want you to get stuck in this Romare rut. I appreciate that you love to collage, but you have to be able to stretch a bit more," she said, swiping my work with her eyes.

"Thank you, Ms. Roberts!" Paulette said enthusiastically as if she wasn't just cutting me with that same tongue two seconds ago. "This was a great trip — better than last year, even."

Somehow, I managed a half smile, but I didn't look up.

With my head bent down, neither Paulette nor Ms. Roberts could see the tear sliding down my cheek.

Chapter Four

"Okay, you've changed your skirt three times, and your hair looks supercute just the way it is," Gabriella whined as she checked her watch. Again. "While you're standing there frowning in the mirror, everybody is at The Spot, eating up all the red velvet cupcakes!"

"So you're saying that stuffing a red velvet cupcake down your throat is more important than how I look when we go to get them?" I asked as I pulled a pair of lavender-and-white polka-dot leggings under my jean miniskirt.

"Don't twist my words, Mina!" Gabriella laughed. "I'm just saying that you look great and it's time for us to get a move on, already."

"Uh-huh," I laughed easily as I stood back to get a good look at myself in the mirror. I twisted my head a little and closed one eye. *Yeah, this outfit just might work.* I kicked my purple Converses out into the middle of the floor, and then swirled around in a circle until I spotted my cute, but uncomfortable, pair of white wedge sandals, and kicked them next to my sneakers. "Converse or sandals?"

"Sneakers," Gabriella said, exasperated. "Can we go now?"

"Who wears sneakers to a fancy restaurant?"'

"Dude, I keep telling you, it's not a fancy restaurant!" Gabriella insisted. "It's a cute little hangout spot where all the kids from the neighborhood go for Poetry Slam Wednesdays. And trust: Nobody's dressing like they're about to pose for *America's Next Top Model.*"

"I just don't want to look like the clueless new girl," I sighed. "I get enough of that at camp to last two lifetimes." At least I'd learned a few things recently, like the location of Pearl Paint — the "Pearl" Gabriella had referred to the day I met her on the subway. Pearl Paint was an amazing art supply store in downtown Manhattan on Canal Street, where Gabriella and I had gone after class to buy new paintbrushes.

"What are you talking about?" Gabriella asked. "I mean, Ms. Roberts really seems to like your art!"

"Whatev," I shot back. "She practically ripped my Picasso to shreds. Anyway, Ms. Roberts isn't the one I meant."

"Mina," Gabriella said, giving me a long look. "Please do not let Paulette get to you. She's not worth it."

I plopped down onto the daybed and stared out the window at the leaves on a huge, gnarled oak twisting in the summer breeze. Yesterday, I'd spent what seemed like hours staring at that tree as I tried to figure out what I needed to do to fit in at camp. Well, specifically, to get Paulette to stop terrorizing me the way she had for the last two weeks. Ever since our unfortunate run-in at the Met, I'd felt pretty low. I hadn't even been able to enjoy the gorgeous, ancient Temple of Dendur or the beautiful Monets and Renoirs we'd looked at in the Impressionist wing. I couldn't stand the fact that someone like Paulette was basically threatening to ruin my summer.

"Thing is, I don't even know what I did to her to make her hate me," I told Gabriella. "What's her deal?"

"She doesn't hate you," Gabriella insisted.

"She's just jealous of you because somebody else in the class is finally getting some shine. She can be so first grade."

"No kidding," I groaned.

"It's nothing new, trust me," Gabriella went on. "She did the same thing to me last year when Ms. Roberts was encouraging me to get bolder with my colors. Honest to goodness, the more bold my paintings got, the meaner Paulette was to me."

"Really?" I asked. I felt bad for Gabriella, but it also made me feel a bit better to know I wasn't alone.

"You know," Gabriella went on thoughtfully, "sometimes I wonder if the only reason Paulette is so evil is because of her home life. Last year, her parents got a divorce, and her dad came to the final art show with a new girlfriend, and then he and Paulette's mom got into a shouting match in front of the whole camp. Paulette was so embarrassed! I would have been, too. My guess is that she's got some serious stuff going on at home, and the only place where she has some control is at our camp. So really, it's all her issue, not yours."

"Wow," I said, taking all this information in. Paulette acted like everything in her life was perfect, but that seemed far from the truth.

"Just be yourself, and ignore Paulette," Gabriella assured me.

I wished it were that easy. I didn't know how to deal with Paulette and be myself all at the same time. I mean, I'd never had a problem being me before, and most everybody back home in Greenwood liked plain ol' Mina. All this extra mess was wearing me out.

Still, I gave Gabriella a grateful look. Just past her shoulder, I caught sight of my chalkboard wall. Earlier, Auntie Jill used a hot-pink pastel to scribble *How I Feel* in a semicircle on the board. Right after camp today, I scribbled *argh!* in the shape of a slithery snake all the way across the wall, because that was how I felt — frustrated. But after my little Gabriella pep talk, I was feeling a bit more hopeful. I walked over to the chalkboard, erased the snake, then picked up a bubblegum-pink pastel, and turned Auntie Jill's words into a smiley face with crossed eyes and a tongue hanging out.

Gabriella giggled. "See? You've been holding out — you're kinda nutty. I like that!"

"Thanks, I guess," I said. "So how do I look?" I asked again, pushing Paulette and art camp from my thoughts.

"Like a rock star," she said.

Just as I slipped the second Converse high-top on, Auntie Jill called up to us: "Okay, ladies, if we keep this pace, we're going to get to The Spot just in time to wash up the dishes and close it down. If we get there and the red velvet cupcakes are gone? Oh, it's going to be a situation!"

"Coming, Auntie!" I yelled down as Gabriella and I bolted for the door. We skipped down the stairs and practically into my aunt's arms. "What's the big deal about these red velvet cupcakes, anyway?" I asked, stopping short, causing Gabriella to bump into my back. We giggled.

Auntie Jill shook her head and sighed. "Seriously? You two have issues. And I'll have you know that those delicious, creamy little red delicacies are quite a big deal, Ms. Missy!" she said. "My goodness, I can taste the cream cheese just standing here. You'll see — if we ever get out of the house!"

Let's just say the words *delicious* and *delicacies* hardly began to describe those cupcakes. *Incredible? Unbelievable? Amazing?* Yes, *amazing* was the word. I'd had red velvet cake before; my grandmother, when she was alive, would make them for special occasions like Thanksgiving and Easter when we celebrated the holidays with them down in Savannah, Georgia. But I was little then, and not too many six-year-olds could appreciate cream cheese frosting. Anyway, I was sure not even my grandmother's red velvet cake could come even close to tasting like the cupcakes in The Spot.

"I have to have another one of these," I said, washing down the last bite of my cupcake with a swig of my mango-banana-strawberry smoothie as I surveyed the room from our table. The café was brightly colored and immediately welcoming, with Day-Glo green walls and orange-and-yellow polka-dot chairs.

"Hey, Mina, maybe you should try eating the red velvets with human bites — you can taste them better that way," Gabriella joked.

"You know, your friend has a point," Auntie Jill laughed.

I exaggerated a frown. "Sheesh, Auntie, I'm family! You're not supposed to cosign with her!"

"I'm just saying. . . ." Auntie Jill said, raising her hands in mock surrender. She reached into her purse and pulled out a crisp five-dollar bill. "Um, and while you're over there getting another one for yourself, bring back enough for the table, 'kay?"

"See?" I said, pushing back from the table.

"Making me out to be greedy. You two aren't any better!"

As I made my way to the coffee counter, I couldn't help but take in the scene. The Spot was, by far, the coolest hangout I'd ever seen. There were all kinds of funky stuff happening. Up on a small stage at the back, a DJ cut and scratched a popular song while a few kids danced to the tunes; over at the table by the front window, a bunch of kids were playing flutes and clarinets. Nearby, three girls were running through a dance routine that Auntie Jill told me they were planning for the upcoming West Indian Labor Day Parade. At the old-fashioned-looking counter, two guys pounded out a beat on the blue Formica while their friends took turns freestyling a rap about Nikes and Brooklyn and some girl named Tameka.

All around the room, kids were laughing and sipping on fruit smoothies and iced coffees and talking animatedly about everything — the latest movies, tennis lessons at Fort Greene Park, who had the best pizza in Clinton Hill, what was going on for the weekend. I'd never seen anything like it. Everybody looked cool and easy — had their own style and swagger about them. It was infectious, and I was so happy to be a part of it.

Seriously: Who knew places like this really existed? The Spot was definitely my new happy place. I couldn't wait to tell Liza and Sam all about it.

"You guys, I got there just in time — these were the last three," I said as I walked up to our table, balancing my newly acquired cupcakes. "But I'm warning you, you better hurry up and eat yours because they're looking mighty tasty, and I may not be able to control . . ."

I stopped mid-sentence when I looked up and saw a boy sitting in my chair.

Gabriella looked at me, and then at the boy, and then back at me again, and smiled. "Hey, Mina, meet my friend Marley. Marley, this is Mina. She and I go to art camp together."

"Hey, what's up?" Marley said, tossing his chin in my direction.

"Hey," I said because I couldn't think of a single, solitary word other than *hey*.

Marley was too cute for words — cuter, dare I say, than even Corbin Bleu. Well, maybe that was going a little far — nobody on the planet is as cute as Corbin. But this boy? Oh. My.

"Oh, hey — I'm in your seat, aren't I," he said, pushing back from the table.

Still no words.

"So, um, your aunt tells me you're visiting from New Jersey?"

"Uh-huh," I said, taking my seat and handing out the cupcakes to my aunt and Gabriella. I said a prayer way on the inside that he didn't notice my hands shaking.

"How are you liking Brooklyn so far?" he continued, taking his shoulder-length locs into his hands and tying them into a low knot, near the nape of his neck.

"It's, um, cool," I said, fiddling with the paper on my cupcake.

"I fear now that she's had the red velvet cupcakes, we're never going to get rid of her," my aunt said. "Good thing we actually like her."

Still, I said nothing.

"So," Gabriella said, trying to break the awkward silence, "are you ciphering today?"

As badly as I wanted to know what ciphering was, I sure wasn't about to ask that stupid question right there, right then. I guessed I'd figure it out eventually.

"You know it," Marley said with a grin. "I'm going to try some new material out. And dig it: My boy Cutz is going to paint onstage while I'm performing. It's going to be kinda hot."

"Sounds like it," my aunt said. "You know, Mina and Gabriella are both artists, too. Maybe one of these days they could accompany you onstage."

"That would be cool," Marley said, smiling right at me. Just as he did so, I grabbed for my smoothie and . . . missed. A small bit of the pink liquid oozed on the table; as I hurriedly reached out, my elbow swiped the top of my red velvet cupcake, and cream cheese icing made a track all the way across my arm. *Embarrassing!*

"Whoa, let me get you some napkins," Marley said.

Before he could get a few steps toward the counter, the DJ got on his mike and cleared his throat. "Okay, party people. It's Poetry Slam Wednesday and I'd like to invite up to the stage a crowd favorite, my dude Marley. And making his performance-painting debut today is my man Cutz, who's going to do an original piece while Marley kicks a verse. Let's give them both a round of applause."

"Oh, gotta get to the stage," Marley said, grabbing a few napkins off an empty table next to ours. "Mina, it was nice meeting you. Next time, save some cupcakes for the rest of us. See you around."

"Yeah, um, see you around," I said, trying to

make myself look too busy cleaning up the mess I'd made to actually look him in the eye.

"I'll text you later," Gabriella said to Marley. "Maybe we can meet up here next week and talk about the performance."

"Yeah — sounds good," Marley said.

Now, I was trying not to crush on the boy, seeing as my aunt was sitting at the table. I didn't need her rushing back to tell my mom about my liking someone, especially since my mom and dad said I couldn't even think about boys until I was sixteen, much less date them. Gabriella knew not to say anything either, but I could tell from the slick grin on her face that we would definitely be discussing Marley when my aunt was out of earshot. For now, though, we both had to be content with watching him up on the stage, busting a rhyme.

He was incredible, too. While the DJ scratched out a crazy beat, Marley leaned into his microphone and spun out an incredible, rhythmic poem about unity. And while he rhymed, Cutz splashed his paint on an oversize canvas that, by the time Marley finished his cipher, revealed itself to be two hands — one black and one white — fingers intertwined, layered atop a rainbow of colors. It was amazing.

When the beats finally stopped and Marley and Cutz took their bows, I was clapping like I was at a Jonas Brothers concert. Don't worry — I wasn't the only one. It seemed Marley and Cutz had that effect on a lot of people — especially all the other girls in the room.

I was still envisioning Marley and Cutz — well, more Marley — when I pulled out my sketch-book back at my aunt's house and tackled my homework assignment from camp. Ms. Roberts's instructions had been really vague: *Sketch something that inspires you,* she had said. Now, in my head, that something could have been anything; rainbows are inspiring. So are mothers. My little sister gets really inspired if you wave a glazed doughnut in her face. But I didn't think Ms. Roberts wanted to see a rainbow or a doughnut in my sketchbook the next day, and I wasn't good enough at drawing faces to whip up a sketch of my mom. But after Marley's performance that evening, I had inspiration to spare.

I flipped to a clean piece of paper and then sat back on the daybed and closed my eyes. I pictured Marley leaning into the microphone, and the way he waved his hands in the air while he pushed out his words; I saw Cutz's paintbrush flying against the canvas, and the DJ's fingers on the record he was spinning. I saw the spilled smoothie slinking across the table, and the red velvet cupcake with the icing missing. Recalling the evening made my heart race a little.

The front doorbell snapped me out of my daze; I could hear my aunt opening the heavy door and having a quick but friendly conversation with whoever rang. "Mina!" she called out after she said her good-byes and closed the door behind her guest. "Could you come downstairs, please?"

"Coming, Auntie," I yelled out as I made my way down the stairs.

"You got a package. It was sent priority mail, and since we were out, the postman left it with the neighbor. Here you go," Auntie Jill said, handing me a blue-and-white square box. "It's from someone named Samantha."

A grin spread across my face from one ear to the other.

"Who's Samantha?" Auntie Jill asked. "Is that one of your girlfriends?"

"Yes!" I said excitedly, shaking the package and examining Samantha's handwriting.

"Well, don't shake it too hard," Auntie said. "There might be something fragile in it."

"Oh, you're right," I said. "Do you have something I can use to open it?"

"Sure, come on into the kitchen. We can open it in there."

Auntie pulled out a couple of kitchen drawers until she found a small X-acto knife; she eased it across the tape on the top of the box, and then used her fingers to pry the flaps open. "There you go," she said, pushing the box across the counter toward me.

I ripped through the purple tissue paper and little foam things and dug down into the box until my hands hit something soft. I pulled it out; it was a rolled-up T-shirt. As I unrolled it, a pair of purple sunglasses and a white shell necklace splashed onto the table. "Oooh! Cute!" I squealed. I put the sunglasses on and held the necklace up to my neck.

"Very pretty," Auntie said, giving it a nod of approval, and then I held up the T-shirt. I cracked up at what it said on the back: It read: I'D RATHER BE SURFING IN SALT ISLE.

"Well, looks like Miss Samantha is quite the shopper and knows your taste, huh?" Auntie said.

"Definitely," I said. "I'm going to go put them away."

My gifts tucked close to my chest, I ran back upstairs and rushed into my room. I looked at Samantha's gifts a few more times, feeling close to my bestie even though she was so far away. I sent her a silent thank-you across the miles for sending me a small piece of the beach. It was on beaches that I always felt powerful, like my connection to the water and the sand and the blue skies gave me superstrength. Just thinking about what mattered most to me — my friends who love me, and the beach, which I love, made me feel so much better about the Paulette situation.

I picked up the picture of me and my best friends. Man, I wished Sam and Liza were here to see all the cool things I was experiencing here in Brooklyn, and even in art camp. They'd think it was pretty incredible, I was sure of it.

I pulled off my sunglasses and put them on the nightstand, along with the necklace, my T-shirt, and the picture, too, and looked at them one more time before I picked up my sketch pad again, wishing that Samantha could have been here to enjoy this. She'd get a kick out of my inspiration painting, for sure.

Chapter Five

"Okay, how'd you do that?" Toby asked, leaning into my inspiration painting; he was close enough for his nose to practically touch the paper. "Is that a bottle cap?"

"Yup," I answered enthusiastically. I stepped back to let him, Gabriella, and a few other people I'd made friends with at camp get a better look. It had taken me three weeknights of nonstop work and an entire Sunday afternoon to complete my picture, and I was pretty pleased with how it turned out. "I thought it would be cool to play with the colors and add in some texture on the knot in the hair," I said. "There's some yarn in it, and some printed paper on it, too. I think it came out kinda cool."

Truth was, I couldn't wait for Ms. Roberts and the other camp instructors to evaluate it in our first art critique. I checked out the other students' easels. Julia, whose work was two easels down from mine, had painted a white basket with bananas in it. And Toya did a sketch of her toy poodle, Willie. I really hoped his eyes weren't crossed like they were in her picture. And Levi had done a pastel drawing of his Nintendo DS. I thought it was pretty funny that a silver handheld video game was his inspiration, but why not?

I felt suddenly nervous. I thought my piece was good, but what if Ms. Roberts preferred everyone else's?

As if on cue, Paulette strolled up, stopped dead center in front of my painting, and stared. Well, more like glared.

"What, exactly, is that a picture of?" she asked, tilting her head to the side.

"It's, uh, a friend of mine I met at The Spot in Fort Greene. It's the back of his head," I said, nowhere near as confidently as I was feeling.

"The back of his head? Hmm," she said.

Just *hmm*.

Argh!

I decided to be the bigger person.

"I, uh, I like yours, too," I said, nodding in the

direction of her easel. On it was a picture of a huge tree in a huge yard in front of a house, gray and stately, with an ornate fence surrounding it. She'd done a lot of work with highlighting and shadows, making the picture, especially the tree, pop off the canvas. I had to admit, it was good. Really good. "The house is pretty."

Paulette looked shocked by my nice response, and I felt a little wave of triumph. Before Paulette could respond, Ms. Roberts strolled into the room and clapped to get our attention.

"Alrighty — let's get started," she said as a handful of counselors from other camp groups within the school lined up behind her. Auntie Jill, who taught painting to sixteen-year-olds upstairs, was there, too. Together, their blue T-shirts looked like a small sea against the sand-brown wall.

"We're going to go easel to easel checking out your work," Ms. Roberts said, "and we're going to listen to how you came about your inspiration. Then we'll give you constructive criticism on how to make it better. Now, it's not easy to let people stand around and say not-so-flattering things about your work; I know this. But I don't want you to take what we say about your work personally. Everything that we're going to tell you will ultimately help you become a better artist. It's not meant to hurt your feelings.

"With that said," Ms. Roberts added as she moved toward the grouping of easels, "let's begin."

Honest to goodness, it was like they were moving in slow motion toward the easels, Ms. Roberts leading the pack. With each step, I reevaluated my decision that morning to pick an easel in the middle of all the others. Maybe I should have made it so that they could look at my work first, so that every other picture after it would pale in comparison. Or maybe I should have tried to be somewhere at the end of the critiques — you know, like, save the best for last. Or maybe I was just thinking about it too hard.

I chewed on one of my nails; my auntie winked at me and sent me a reassuring smile, which gave me great comfort. She, after all, had been a big help while I completed my assignment; she was the one who suggested I add the ribbon and paper to give my picture texture. And she was pretty honest about a few of my earlier drafts, which, after she said they seemed "uninspired," found a nice home in her compost bin, beneath her coffee grounds, my tea bags, and a handful of orange peels and half-squeezed lemons she tossed in to help make the homemade fertilizer she kept for her container garden. She didn't have to tell me twice when something stunk.

But she'd liked this version. At the very least, she'd stick up for me, right? Knowing this helped settle the butterflies swarming in my stomach.

Poor Julia got evaluated first. "This is, um, interesting," Ms. Roberts said. "I'm kind of curious about why you would do a white basket against white paper. The color treatment makes your work melt into the white background."

Julia's shoulders fell a mile. She tried to defend herself. "The basket is white and it's on the table in our kitchen. It's white, too."

"I see. But there had to be a way to distinguish between the different shades of white so that you could tell where the basket ends and the table begins," Ms. Roberts said as the other counselors leaned into her work. Auntie Jill patted Julia, now officially defeated, on her shoulder. "This is a really nice start," Ms. Roberts concluded, "but I think you should go back in and find a way to make your subject stand out more."

"Okay," was all Julia could manage.

Ms. Roberts moved on to Gabriella's easel. I'd been hanging out with her long enough to tell that when she shook her hair out, she was nervous. When she was especially embarrassed, her cheeks and forehead turned a particular shade of scarlet red, like the color of a reddish brown leaf on a tree in the fall. Sort of the color her face was when Ms. Roberts came to a stop in front of her.

"Well, Gabriella, why don't you tell me about your artwork," Ms. Roberts began.

"I did a close-up of a pot of flowers my mom keeps in her container garden out on the front stoop of our brownstone," she said. "I love the color."

"It is a nice color," Auntie Jill chimed in.

"Yes, it is," Ms. Roberts cosigned. "But I wonder if you could have put a little bit more effort into the container and the building in the background. That would make the color pop even more. Try that and see where it goes. Overall, nice job."

"I'll do that," Gabriella said, not the least bit fazed by the criticism. She'd been at the camp before and maybe that made it a little easier for her to take it. "Thank you."

Ms. Roberts praised and shamed her way through six more campers before she finally stood in front of my easel, squinting at my artwork. I bit my lip waiting for the verdict. My blueberry vanilla lip gloss tasted like wax, but I chewed on, anyway.

"Mina, I've been looking forward to critiquing your work, seeing as you clearly come from a family of talented artists," Ms. Roberts said, nodding at Auntie Jill. "I know I've kept a watchful eye over your in-class assignments, but this is your first big critique. Are you ready?"

"I, um, I think . . . yeah," I stuttered.

"Well, then," Ms. Roberts said, leaning into my easel. "Tell me about it."

This part, I hadn't been expecting. How was I supposed to stand there in the middle of a class full of people and tell them that I was inspired to draw my picture after meeting a cute boy? How would I have sounded, talking about how I'd spent the last week drawing a picture of some boy's hair?

No. Way.

"It's a picture, um, of, um . . . my hair," I stuttered.

"Hmm. Well, the color is a little off, no?" she asked, leaning in. My locs are reddish brown. Marley's are a beautiful brownish gold, like Corbin's.

"I wanted to play with the colors a little," I

answered quickly. "I thought reddish brown would be a little boring."

I shot a look in Paulette's direction just as she elbowed Mariska and gave her a lopsided grin. *Please, please, please don't say anything,* I thought to myself. The last thing I needed was for everyone in the class to know my inspiration was some boy who barely knew I existed. Not even Gabriella knew the drawing was of Marley's locs, even though she was the one who introduced us. He was her friend. I got a mental image of myself walking into The Spot and seeing Gabriella whispering to Marley that I was some crazed stalker girl who spent practically a week's worth of evenings drawing and painting his hair.

This was *so* a conversation I didn't want to have.

"But I thought . . ." Paulette began.

I cleared my throat, hoping that she'd drop it, and keep what I'd told her about my picture to herself. No such luck. Paulette went in for the kill.

"But didn't you tell me earlier that it was the back of some boy's head?" she asked with an icy smile.

I forced a smile back, and stared down at my Converses, mortified that Paulette had just busted me. Why did I have to open my big mouth and tell her about the boy anyway? "I meant, um . . . I was trying . . ." I stuttered.

"It's a combination," Gabriella chimed in. "See? You can tell it's styled like her locs, but the color is like our friend's hair. I think it looks kinda cool."

"Yeah, um, that's kinda what I was doing. My inspiration was hair in general," I emphasized. "Not the hair of any specific person."

I gave the evil eye to Paulette, who responded with a nose scrunch and whispered to Mariska. Ms. Roberts was totally oblivious to the theater unfolding before her; she was too busy studying my painting.

Finally, she pulled back from the painting. "Nice approach," she said, making me breathe a sigh of relief. "This class is about learning, but also innovation," she added. "I think what you've done with the ribbon and paper is interesting, and you're headed in the right direction. I want you to keep at this. You still need to figure out how to express yourself as an artist. You're not there yet, but this is a nice start."

I nodded.

"Good job," Ms. Roberts said, patting me on the back as she moved on to the next easel. Auntie

Jill gave me a wink and a rub on my back and moved on, too.

I simply stared at my picture. Honestly, I couldn't tell if she liked it or thought it was childish. A nice start? Suddenly, I wasn't feeling all that inspired. In fact, I didn't know if I was supposed to hang the painting up on the wall and be proud of it, or let Auntie Jill run it over with her car.

"And last but not least, Paulette," I heard Ms. Roberts say a little too enthusiastically for my taste. She leaned into Paulette's easel and smiled. "A tree! Quite a nice one, might I add."

"It's the tree in front of my father's house in the Hamptons," Paulette said. "I drew it because I can see it right outside my window in the bedroom I sleep in when I stay with him."

"Well, I love the movement of the leaves. It looks like they're fluttering in the wind. And you did it in watercolors. Very classic. Nice job, Paulette."

"Thank you," she said, smiling at her picture as if she were admiring herself in a mirror. When Ms. Roberts turned her back, Paulette high-fived her girls, and tossed a smirk in my direction for good measure. Clearly, she was pleased with herself. I was not.

I *was* thoroughly embarrassed. I felt like an idiot for walking into camp like I was Picasso, and being dissed like I'd brought in a third grade finger painting. In fact, I wondered if Ms. Roberts probably would have given me a better critique if I *had* come with something childish.

And how I was going to explain my Marley crush to Gabriella?

"Okay, everyone, I need you to take a seat on the rug so we can talk about your next in-class project," Ms. Roberts said, snapping me out of my daze.

My fellow students dutifully made their way to the front of the class, giggling and whispering to one another as if the massive slaughter that just went down didn't happen. I've never been that quick about getting over such things. So I took my time digging for imaginary art supplies in my bag, with the hope that moving slowly would leave me no choice but to sit in the back and sulk a little.

Before I realized what was going on, Gabriella was grabbing my hand and pulling me toward the door. "Ms. Roberts — we're just going to take a quick bathroom break," she called out to our camp instructor. She didn't give her a chance to respond — she just yanked me through the door and down the hall into the tiny two-stall bathroom. She hurriedly peeked into both stalls like she was on some kind of secret mission, and then she turned to me.

"Omigod — why didn't you tell me you like Marley?" she said excitedly, shaking out her hands and jumping up and down a little.

"What?" I asked, playing like I was clueless. "Marley? I . . . don't like Marley," I stuttered.

"Mina! You so don't give that level of paint detail to someone you don't have some kind of crush on. Girl, why didn't you tell me? Marley is my homie — I could totally see him liking you . . . and I could even set something up. . . ."

"Gabriella, seriously . . ." I began, feeling my face get hot.

"Man, why didn't I pick up on this? My radar is so totally better than that. . . ." she continued, talking to herself like I wasn't in the room.

"Gabriella!" I yelled. My voice bounced off the yellow tiles and practically yelled back at us. "Please stop," I said slowly. "I'm not even thinking about Marley right now. Some inspiration he turned out to be."

"What are you talking about? He was perfect. Look at the picture you came up with," Gabriella said.

"Ms. Roberts didn't like it," I said, pouting. "At all."

"Oh, come on, Mina," she said. "Harsh much? You act like she wanted to drive a stake through it."

"Um, were you even in the same room as me? Even if all she had was a butter knife, she would have stabbed the painting a dozen times if she could."

"You know what? You're right — maybe we weren't in the same room. Because what I heard from our camp instructor was that she liked what you did. I know I at least heard her say 'good work,'" Gabriella said, tucking a stray sandy-brown curl behind her left ear and running her fingers over her thick eyebrows.

"Yeah, after she basically told me it sucked," I said, sulking. "And I swear, Paulette is making it even worse."

Gabriella turned from the mirror and looked at me. "Okay, you've got to stop this."

"Stop what?" I asked.

"You're letting Paulette drive you batty," she said.

"Well, you have to admit, she is making camp feel like an enemy zone," I insisted, folding my arms.

"Look, she's competitive and she's not going to make winning the big end-of-camp prize easy. But your work is totally incredible. Everybody else can see that. Why can't you?" she asked as she backed away from me and toward the bathroom door. "You have to stop letting Paulette get into your head. Seriously."

And with that, she disappeared down the hall and back into class.

I took a look at myself in the mirror and adjusted the purple bandanna holding back my locs. *She's right, you know,* I told myself. *Get your head in the game.*

When I got back into the classroom, Ms. Roberts was already well into her lesson about Faith Ringgold. "What's incredible about this artist is her use of words," Ms. Roberts said as I took a seat on the rug between Gabriella and Toby. "She doesn't just create pictures. Each piece of art has a story painted directly onto it, so the story, in essence, comes to life. Today, your challenge is to create a work of art and, like Ringgold, pair it with words that tell a story about your painting."

Hushed conversation washed over the room as everyone started thinking out loud about what they might want to draw. Gabriella got up and stretched and yawned. "Ooh, I'm going to draw lunch, because I'm starving," she said, rolling her head in circles to work the kinks out of her neck.

"Mmm — I can see it now: Lombardi's, the table in the back, a mushroom-and-olive pie," Toby laughed. "And I think I just officially made myself hungry."

Gabriella laughed as we grabbed our fabric and moved toward our easels. "You know it! My words will be an ode to Lombardi's pizza. Maybe I'll write 'sweet and extra cheesy' all around the border."

"Well, the 'extra cheesy' part would be spot-on," Paulette said, strolling by with a giggly Mariska and the always-attitudinal Stephanie close on her heels.

Gabriella frowned, but she kept her thoughts to herself, which, of course, signaled Paulette to dig in a little more. She trained her eyes on me. "And, um, let me guess: You'll be drawing The Spot, right? Maybe with your friend with the black — no, brown . . . or was it black and brown hair?" She shook her head, giggled, and walked away. And right at that moment, I was so officially over her and her little friends and especially that camp. Forget pizza and The Spot and especially Paulette. I was in serious need of a Samantha and Liza intervention — one that could be had at the Greenwood public pool, in our special spot, a few feet from the lifeguard station. My best friends would think my painting was cool, and they wouldn't make a big deal about Marley. They'd understand that I thought he was cute but that was it. I wasn't even sure how I felt about boys in general just yet.

I felt like an alien in New York City. But back at the pool, sitting on my favorite deck chair, lying on my favorite towel and listening to the kids of Greenwood splashing around in the water, I was at home. Liza and Sam just got me.

I clipped my white handkerchief on my easel and then reached down for my pencil. I knew exactly what I'd draw on it: a picture of me in my favorite purple swimsuit, chilling out with my best friends on the beach in Cape May. On the edges of my picture, I planned to write the words: *Choice waves, good friends, peace, and love.*

In other words, things I didn't think existed here in New York City.

Chapter 6

I ran a mental checklist of things Liza told me to do to look more like a New Yorker and less like a tourist when I visited Manhattan: *Keep your head down, walk straight and fast because New Yorkers get really mad when people who aren't from New York get in their way, and never, ever, under any circumstances, look up at the skyscrapers.*

Do that, and you might as well have the word *tourist* scribbled across your forehead. At least that was what Liza's dad had told her. He worked in Manhattan.

I tried to keep this advice in mind as our class made our way up the staircase leading out of the subway and into the bright sun washing over

Rockefeller Center. But it wasn't easy. Every building, every billboard, every window was like candy to my eyes.

"Last year we went to Takashimaya to check out Japanese water prints, and we saw Vanessa Hudgens and Ashley Tisdale just walking down the street like normal people," Gabriella whispered as she grabbed my hand. "They had shopping bags and a bunch of guys with cameras were following them and everybody was staring. It was crazy!"

"Do you think there'll be celebrities over here?" I asked excitedly as we made our way up Fifth Avenue, my eyes straying from all the fancy jewelry shops and clothing stores to search the oncoming crowd. Maybe Corbin would be shopping in Armani. Or buying a nice diamond necklace for his mom at Tiffany. I peered through the window, totally looking for Corbin, totally not noticing the ocean's worth of pearls in the window display. "I have my camera with me."

"It's not really cool to take their pictures," said Gabriella. "Mostly, around here people just ignore celebrities, except for the professional camera guys."

"Well, I don't want to look like a tourist, but if I

look up and see Corbin Bleu walking toward me, it might get a little crazy around here — I'm just saying!"

Gabriella laughed as we picked up our pace to keep up with the rest of the class. I kept scanning the faces of the people walking toward me. There was no Corbin Bleu or Vanessa Hudgens or anyone famous — just regular people swarming the streets with their briefcases and their fast-food bags and their Starbucks cups. None of them seemed to pay their surroundings any mind. As for me? I couldn't help but to sneak a peek toward the sky when Ms. Roberts led us to the front of a beautiful, cream-colored building.

"This building is the Plaza, and it used to be a really famous hotel," Ms. Roberts announced. "People now live in apartments here. Have any of you ever read the book *Eloise*?" she asked.

I tried not to be a cornball about it, but *Eloise* was totally my favorite when I was into picture books. Eloise was a nut and always got herself into some kind of mess, and never ever got in trouble for it. What kid wouldn't sign up for that? I still sneak and read them when my little sister leaves her Eloise books lying around. I wonder if you really can slide down the laundry shoot into a big pile of sheets in a secret room somewhere, and if the guy in the black suit really does bring you whatever you want whenever you want if you just call him on the phone.

"And we're also right near Central Park," Ms. Roberts added, pointing to the cluster of vivid green trees. Horse-drawn carriages were lined up in front of the park. "For those of you who are new to New York, Central Park is our city's most famous park, and it has countless beautiful spots. Very inspiring. And just across Fifth Avenue is one of the most famous toy stores in the world," Ms. Roberts continued, pointing at FAO Schwarz. "Any of you ever see the movie *Big*, about the kid who turns into an adult?"

We all nodded enthusiastically.

"You remember the scene where he and his boss are playing 'Chopsticks' on the gigantic floor piano? Well, this is the store with that giant piano."

We let out a chorus of "oohs" and "aahs."

"Okay, okay, simmer down because I want you guys to have plenty of time for your assignment, which is to find your idea of a classic New York scene and sketch it. Now, I'm going to break you all up into pairs so that you have a buddy to work with. The two of you will be responsible for deciding together what to draw, sketching your own versions of it, and, most important, looking out for each other while we're out here doing our work. I know a lot of you are familiar with New York City, but we still need to be careful about where you all go, so no wandering. I need you to stay somewhere within a three-block radius of FAO Schwarz.

"So," she added, looking at her watch, "let's get you into pairs."

Gabriella and I naturally moved close to each other because it was a no-brainer that we wanted to work together. But Ms. Roberts put the kibosh on that with a quickness; she'd already made a list and was calling out the pairs she'd put together in advance.

I wrinkled my brow when she called out Gabriella's name with Stephanie's. I got nervous when she called out a few more names and Toby got paired with a boy named Scott Grey. When the last two campers standing ended up being me and Paulette, I almost gagged.

"Wait — there must be some mistake," Paulette insisted, waving her hand. "Um, I'm with Mina?"

Ms. Roberts looked down at her paper, and said simply, "Yes."

Both Paulette and I got looks on our faces like someone had thrown cold water on us. But before either of us could protest, Ms. Roberts hammered out her instructions: "We've got an hour to get our sketches done and meet back by the fountain in front of the Plaza."

It would be the longest hour of my entire twelve years on the earth. I was sure of it.

I mean, it's not that I was scared of Paulette or anything. It's just that I didn't prepare myself for any drama that day. My auntie had been coaching me on how to handle Paulette, and the lesson always began and ended with Auntie Jill saying, "Just ignore her." I'd done a pretty good job of it over the last week since the first art critique; even when she "accidentally" spilled her paintbrush water all around my easel just as I was picking up my art-supplies bag, I didn't get upset or flustered. I just stepped out of the way while Ms. Roberts dabbed at the water, and Paulette stood around, acting like she was helping, but wasn't really.

But working with her? For an entire hour? Alone?

Ugh.

"Okay, let's get to it!" Ms. Roberts said.

The pairs scattered; Gabriella shrugged her shoulders as she walked by with Stephanie. "Good luck with that," she whispered, nodding her head in Paulette's direction.

"Good grief, I can't believe Ms. Roberts," Paulette said, crossing her arms and pouting.

"Can't believe what?" I asked, mimicking her stance.

"I can't believe she stuck me with you," she said. "Unless she meant to put good artists with bad ones. Yeah, maybe that's it — she wants me to show you how it's done."

"I don't need your help," I replied curtly. "We only have one hour to get our sketches done, and if you don't mind, I'd like to just go ahead and work. But if you're going to insult me, then there's really no point in doing this at all."

I was surprised at how firm I sounded; I'd never expected myself to fight back like that. Paulette looked surprised, too. She blinked a few times, and then collected herself.

"Well, we need to get the assignment done," she said, ever the good student. "So let's just get this over with. I say we cross the street and draw the FAO building."

I took a step back and surveyed the building. It was pretty, with a bunch of glass and some neat lines that could make the artwork interesting. But I wasn't all that impressed. "It's kinda boring," I said, looking at the building sideways.

"Whatever," she said, tossing up a flat hand. "I think drawing the building is a great idea, and seeing as *you* don't have any ideas, let's just run with mine, shall we?"

"You never asked what I want to do," I pointed out.

"Because I don't really care," she said sweetly, smiling.

"Alrighty, then," I said, exasperated. "How about this: You write down three things you want to sketch, I'll write down three things I want to sketch, and then we'll put them onto little pieces of paper and pick one. That's fair."

"Negative," she said without hesitation.

"Well, maybe we can just run my idea by Ms. Roberts," I said, turning in the direction where our camp instructor was walking. "She can straighten this disagreement right on out."

"Whoa, whoa, hey — no need to engage the adults," Paulette said, grabbing me by the arm.

"A change of heart?" I asked, feeling a little bit more powerful.

"Just write your ideas down so we can do this," she said, reaching into her backpack for a piece of paper.

I gazed at the street again, this time paying

attention not only to the buildings, but to what was happening all around them. The buildings were beautiful, that was true, but what was really catching my attention were the people who were making the street come alive. So, on my slips of paper, I wrote: *little girl walking through the revolving door at the Plaza; a mom blowing bubbles with baby in the stroller; and man and lady reading map near FAO Schwarz.* I handed my slips of paper to Paulette, who, already finished jotting down her notes, was impatiently tapping her foot.

"Okay, I'll pick," she said.

"Why do you get to pick?" I asked.

"Come on, are you kidding? You're standing right there watching me — what, you don't trust me?"

"Well . . ." I shrugged.

"Whatever. Toby!" she yelled out to our fellow camper, who was standing not too far away from us with Scott, making a square with his fingers like he was taking a picture of a horse-drawn carriage. Paulette's loud voice made him jump. "We need you!" she yelled some more.

Toby jogged over to us. "What's up?" he asked.

"Pick one," Paulette said, pushing the folded pieces of paper toward Toby.

He dutifully grabbed one and waved it in the air. "What's this?"

"Thanks, Toby — that's all," Paulette said, shooing Toby away. I grinned at him. He shook his head and jogged back to his spot next to Scott. Paulette opened the slip of paper and grimaced. "What does drawing a mom blowing bubbles with her kid have to do with New York City?" she huffed.

"Yes!" I said, pumping my fist in the air. That was the one I really wanted to do.

"Um, hello? Bubbles? Seriously?"

"Come on, Paulette, drawing a tall building is neat and would probably look like a good New York City scene, but I think the people are cool, too. I'm going to draw the buildings in the background — it'll definitely look like New York City by the time I finish."

Paulette rolled her eyes.

"I'm just saying, we should both go ahead and get the sketch in before that lady stops blowing bubbles and leaves."

Paulette rolled her eyes again and hoisted herself onto the concrete wall of the Plaza fountain and, without another word, started sketching. I took a seat next to her, and we both worked for the next fifty minutes in total silence. First, I sketched the woman and her kid; after they left, I filled in my picture with the background — streetlamps, the sidewalk, the buildings, and cars on the street. When our fifty minutes were up, I held my sketch at arm's length and took a final look at my work.

"Yeah," I said, nodding and smiling. I felt good about my picture. Really good. When I leaned over to get a look at Paulette's work, she slammed her sketchbook closed and rolled her eyes again. I resisted telling her that if she kept doing that, her eyes were going to get stuck in the back of her head.

"Okay," I said slowly. I noticed that Ms. Roberts was beckoning to the other campers. "Looks like everyone's meeting back up. We should probably head over, too."

"She's going to think our sketches are horrible," Paulette sighed. "Mine doesn't look anything like a scene of New York City. If she totally hates it, I'm blaming you," she added as she walked up to the crowd of students gathered around Ms. Roberts.

I sighed and followed, figuring that anything I said would be a total waste of breath.

"Please pass up your work to me so we can all see what you've been doing for the past hour,"

Ms. Roberts said. When she had all of the sketchbooks in hand, she started flipping through and critiquing the pictures. Most of what she said was positive, with the exception of her critique of Zion's and Bill's sketches of a horse's tail. "I'm afraid it doesn't really feel like New York City to me," she said, wrinkling her brow.

"Come on!" Zion said. "Horses? Central Park? They're always pooping in the street? That's New York big-time!"

"Okay, then," Ms. Roberts laughed. "I guess I was looking for something a little more authentic. Just a little," she said.

Paulette leaned in and whispered in my ear: "See? She's going to think the whole blowing bubbles thing isn't New York City. It's all your fault."

"Well!" Ms. Roberts exclaimed as she opened Paulette's sketchbook. "Now, this is the perfect example of showing an original, fresh rendering of New York City. I love how you made the buildings a backdrop to the action on the city street. Great energy — good job, Paulette!" she said, handing the sketchbook back to her.

"Why, thank you!" Paulette said, waving her hands and acting like she was receiving some kind of award. "I thought it was more important to show the people of New York City and not just the buildings. They're the ones that bring life to the city."

I whipped myself around and stared at Paulette in disbelief. She was taking credit for my idea!

"Well, that was a terrific way of looking at it," Ms. Roberts said. "Let that be an example to the rest of you on how to take fresh perspectives on traditional artwork."

I let out a huge sigh — loud enough to turn a few heads. I wanted to scream, *"She stole my idea!"* but I couldn't get the words out.

And I could barely pay attention when Ms. Roberts came to my drawing and said I'd done a good job as well. It didn't matter. Paulette had made it seem like I had nothing to do with finding the lady with the bubbles. I snapped my head in her direction and prepared to give her a few choice words, but she was already up and moving — laughing with Stephanie and Mariska like it wasn't anything for her to tell a lie. My mouth was still hanging wide-open as we all started making our way back to the subway. I was walking double time.

"What's wrong, Mina? You just got a great critique," Gabriella said, trying her best to keep up with me.

"Nothing," I said.

"Come on, Mina. Paulette did something to you, didn't she? What'd she do? You can tell me," Gabriella said.

Honestly? I didn't want to pour my heart out to Gabriella, or yell at Paulette, or stomp down the street like a crazy girl. Actually, I didn't know what I wanted to do. If I told Gabriella what just happened, she might confront Paulette, and who knew where that would lead? And if I told Ms. Roberts, I'd just sound like a tattletale. If I went straight to Paulette, she just might dismiss me, and I'd only get madder. I wished Samantha and Liza were with me. This would have never happened if I weren't stuck there by myself, trying to figure out everybody and everything on my own.

What was worse was that I couldn't even get in touch with my girls; it wasn't like I could just pick up the phone or e-mail them or tell them to meet me so we could talk it out and come up with a plan. I was stuck at that camp another two weeks with Paulette dogging me and, worse, having our camp instructor completely ignore all of my hard work. How was I supposed to even stand a chance of winning the final art competition this way?

Man, what I would have done to be able to hear Samantha's and Liza's voices right then. I reached into my art bag and pulled out the necklace Sam had given me; I'd kept it in my art bag for good luck. If ever I needed it, it was right then.

"Mina," Gabrielle said. Then louder, "Mina!"

"What?" I snapped.

"Do you want to talk about it?" she asked.

"Not really," I said simply. "I'm okay. It's cool."

We descended the steps to the subway in silence, me with my head down, staring at my purple Converses. Corbin Bleu could have been walking toward me blowing kisses, and I wouldn't have seen him.

And right about then, I didn't care either.

Chapter Seven

"Seriously? You've never Double Dutched? Ever?" Gabriella asked as she and another one of her neighborhood friends, Lilly, tossed two ropes between both hands. Another girl, Sierra, bounced back and forth, waiting for the perfect opening to hop in.

"No," I said from the stoop of my auntie's brownstone, where I was sitting with my chin in my hands, my face toward the sun.

It was only eleven A.M., and was superhot outside. The sun's rays beat down on my face, reminding me of the pool back home; I pictured myself lying back on my favorite oversize purple towel, Samantha to my right, Liza to my left, the three of us listening to the water splash and talking about nothing. I really wished I were there.

But nope—I was on the stoop, watching Gabriella and her friends play a game I couldn't figure out how to play, no matter how many times I'd watched Corbin in *Jump In*. I had even convinced my mom to buy me two jump ropes, and then gotten Liza and Sam to watch the "how to Double Dutch" part of *Jump In* before the three of us had headed out to my driveway and had given it a try. Let's just say I ended up tangled in those ropes enough times to figure out I wouldn't be winning any Double Dutch contests anytime soon. We fell out giggling and tossed those ropes in the corner of my garage, where they're collecting dust to this day.

Gabriella and her girls did look like they were having fun, though — singing rhymes and giggling and showing off their moves in front of the crowd of kids gathered around, waiting their turn between the ropes. It was a scene that would never get played out in my neighborhood back in Greenwood. There, my sister and I were almost always one of only a handful of African-American kids wherever we went — at the pool, in the local camp, in school. As much as my parents tried to make sure that we felt comfortable in our own skin and knew our proud history, at the end of the day, the lack of diversity in our neighborhood did force us to miss out on the cool rituals black kids the world over got to experience when they grew up around a mass of other kids who looked, talked, acted like, and came from the same background as them. Some days, I didn't worry about it too much. Other days, like these, the differences were glaring.

"Come on," Gabriella said. "We'll teach you."

"Nah, I'm just chillin' and enjoying the sun," I said, as I scooted over to let the mail lady make her way up to Auntie's mailbox.

"Try it, Mina," Gabriella insisted. "What's it going to hurt to try?"

I looked over at the two girls turning the rope doubly fast and watched a third do a rhythmic bounce between both feet as the three started singing their Double Dutch rhyme:

My mother, your mother lived across the way
Two-four-six East Broadway
Every night they had a fight and this is what
they'd say . . .

The jumper went on for what seemed like an eternity, her lightning-fast feet weaving between the air and the ropes, touching neither, floating between space and time and, of course, on the beat. Always on the beat.

Gabriella didn't wait for me to turn her down again; she simply grabbed my hand and practically pulled me down the brownstone steps onto the street.

"KeKe," she said, addressing one of the turners. "Let me get a turn so I can show my girl Mina how it's done."

"Go for it," KeKe said, effortlessly stepping out of the turning ropes.

"Okay, so the point is to jump in, stay under the rope, and jump to the beat. If you make it through the song, you make it to another round. If you step on the rope, you're out," Gabriella said. "Jumping is easier than it looks. All you have to do is jump in when there's an opening and the rope farthest away from you hits the ground. And then as the ropes come down, just jump over them — exactly like you do with just one rope."

Then, with the greatest of ease, she slipped between the ropes and jumped as gracefully as an Alvin Ailey dancer.

Ice cream, soda pop
Cherries on top

How many boyfriends have you got?
Is it A, B, C, D . . .

I looked at Gabriella like she was speaking another language from a faraway land. After one verse, she hopped out just as easily as she hopped in.

"Well," she said, "go ahead. Try it."

I looked at Gabriella and then the ropes, and back at Gabriella. I felt a huge pang of nerves.

"Come on," she encouraged. "You can do it."

So I watched the ropes, keeping my eye on the "opening" Gabriella swore would magically reveal itself. It didn't. All I could see were two ropes ready to tangle up in my Converses. But it was too late for me to back down; the rope turners looked like they were getting impatient, and Gabriella wasn't exactly ready to say, *Never mind; you don't have to do it.*

So I bounced and looked and bounced some more, and then hurled myself into the ropes and . . . fell. Into one heaping, ugly pile of purple Converses, hot-pink skorts, flying brownish red locs, and beige rope. It. Was. Ugly.

"Omigosh," Gabriella said, holding her hand over her mouth. I couldn't tell if she was stifling a laugh or genuinely shocked at my clumsiness.

"Wow, so I know they don't Double Dutch in New Jersey, but are they short on rhythm, too?" KeKe laughed.

"Come on!" Gabriella said, whipping her head around to admonish KeKe. "That's mean."

I collected myself from the sidewalk, brushed off the dirt from my knees, and slowly walked up the steps to my aunt's brownstone. "It's okay. Like I said, I'm not much of a jump roper," I said quietly, fighting back tears. "Anyway, I'll see you guys around."

"But wait. . . ." Gabriella started. The slamming of Auntie's ornate mahogany door drowned out whatever else she was saying.

I tried to gather my composure before I went to Auntie's kitchen; I didn't want her to see me upset — or, more specifically, to know why I was upset. I really didn't have it in me to explain why I was the only black girl in the world who couldn't Double Dutch and didn't know the jump rope songs. Or that I was scared of being the out-of-touch Jersey girl in the big, bad, fast city — scared of the subway, and clueless about all of the rich culture the city had to offer. No, this I didn't feel like explaining to Auntie Jill. I needed to talk to one of my friends. My real friends.

I found Auntie in the kitchen, hunched over

her lesson plan book. “Auntie, do you think I can use your computer to send my friend Sam an e-mail?” I said, fighting the quiver in my voice.

“She has Internet access?” my aunt questioned absentmindedly, a little distracted by her work at hand. I’d told Auntie Jill about both Liza’s and Sam’s trips that summer.

“Well, I know Liza has no e-mail access, but there’s a small chance Sam might be able to check it,” I explained. “Plus, I want to thank her for her gift.”

“Well, it’s worth a try, sweetie. Of course you can use the computer. Let me log you in,” Auntie said. She rose up from her perch to walk over to her desktop computer on a small table in the living room. I followed her, secretly wiping tears from my eyes while her back was turned.

“Okay, here you go,” Auntie said. “I’m going to go upstairs and throw on a little lipstick and my shoes so that I can run up to the Studio Museum in Harlem for my meeting. You have about five minutes before we have to leave, okay?”

“Okay, Auntie. I’ll be ready,” I called out to her as she walked away. And then I turned my attention back to the computer, typed in Sam’s e-mail addy, and got to work.

Hi Sam,

First of all, thank you for the supercute gift! I feel like I have a piece of the beach — and you! — with me. I wish I could talk to you face-to-face. I really miss you and Liza. Summer isn't the same without you guys, and I could really stand to have you both here.

I met this really cool girl named Gabriella. She lives around the corner from my aunt and goes to the same art camp with me. I think you would like her. She's definitely the bright spot. I can't say that for some of the other people around here, though. I'm just not like them, and trust me, they make a point of reminding me every time they get a chance. Like Paulette, who keeps saying and doing the meanest things possible to make herself look good in front of the instructor. I guess she thinks that the more she puts down my artwork, the more chance she'll have of winning the final art critique. At this point, I don't think I have any kind of chance of winning. I'm counting the days to when we'll be together again in Greenwood.

Miss you,

Mina

I pushed the SEND button just as Auntie Jill made her way down the stairs. "Okay, Mina, I'm running a little late — let's get a move on," she called out.

I took one last look at Sam's name on the computer screen and then clicked SHUT DOWN. "Coming, Auntie," I called out as enthusiastically as I could.

But I was far from happy.

If I weren't in such a funky mood, I'd have thought I was in heaven at the Studio Museum in Harlem. There were paintings and photographs, collages and 3-D art pieces — some of it created by artists my auntie helped me fall in love with, like Elizabeth Catlett, Ann Tanksley, and Kehinde Wiley, and plenty of others I'd never heard of before. The rooms were bursting with color and energy as a handful of art lovers meandered through the halls, stopping to discover the artwork displays and read the tiny info boards about the pieces. My aunt did her best to get me excited about what I was seeing — to remind me that I was a part of the legacy of many wonderful artists of color who were intent on using their art and their incredible talent to show the world how beautiful and diverse and magnificent our people are.

But seeing all the art up close just reminded me that I've got a long way to go to be that good. Plainly put, I felt like I lacked that gene that gave my artwork the passion that made the artwork in the Studio Museum in Harlem worthy of being there. I couldn't imagine making art as beautiful as that which I was looking at right then, and it just reminded me that Paulette was out to prove she was better than me; this just reminded me that the art competition was only two weeks away and I still didn't know what I'd be creating to compete.

Not even seeing an original collage by Romare Bearden could remove me from my worry and funk.

"I thought you loved Bearden," Auntie said, alternately staring at me and the artist's picture of two women in a kitchen, one of whom appeared to be standing in a tub of water.

"I do," I said simply, leaning into the collage to make it look like I was super-interested in it.

"Well, what do you like most about it?"

"Um," I said, hesitating. "It's really colorful?"

Silence.

"That's it?" my aunt finally asked.

"And the paper layers look cool," I said. "It's interesting."

"Interesting?" Auntie asked, wrinkling her brow. She leaned in closer to me, startling me.

"Look, Mina, I'm going to need you to snap out of it, honey."

"What do you mean, Auntie?" I asked innocently. "I said I like the collage."

"Mina, you've barely been paying attention. You're in the middle of one of the most famous museums for art created by artists of color, and you're staring at an original piece by *the* Romare Bearden — something most artists your age who come from where you come from don't get to see often. And all you have to offer is 'It's interesting'?"

"I . . . I like . . ." I began.

"What's wrong, honey?" Auntie asked, her tone much softer now. "Are you homesick?"

I looked down at my lucky Converses. They hadn't really brought me much luck lately; I was really considering simply calling them my sneakers. "No, not really."

"Well, is it that you don't like staying with me in Brooklyn?"

"Oh, gosh, no," I said quickly. "I love staying with you, Auntie Jill. You're, like, the coolest aunt a girl could ever have."

"Well, then what's the problem?" she asked. "You've been walking around the house the last couple of days like a total grump-a-lump, and I need to know how to get you out of this funk."

"It's no big deal, Auntie," I said, still staring at my feet.

Auntie took my chin into her hand and lifted my face up so that my eyes could meet hers. "Little girl, I've changed your diapers, twisted your hair, taken you shopping, babysat you, and vacationed with you, too. I know you — maybe even better than you know yourself. You've never been very good at hiding your feelings. Now, if something's wrong, you need to tell me so that I can maybe help you make it better."

I tried to avert my eyes away from Auntie's, but she had a kung fu grip on my chin and wouldn't let go.

My eyes started to water as I started to explain what had gotten me in a twist.

"I really miss my friends," I began.

Auntie didn't say anything, only watched me with her wide eyes.

"And art camp is a little different from what I expected it to be," I continued.

Still more silence.

"And that girl Paulette keeps giving me a hard time," I added. "Yesterday, when we got paired up for an assignment? I came up with a great idea for what we should do together, and when Ms. Roberts told the whole class she liked it, Paulette told everybody *she* was the one who suggested it!"

"And what did you say when she did that?" Auntie Jill said, finally releasing my chin.

"What do you mean, what did I say?" I questioned.

"What did you say when Paulette took credit for your idea?" Auntie asked simply.

"I didn't say anything. It was the middle of class and I didn't want to cause a fuss," I said.

"Who says you would have had to cause a scene?"

"Well, if I said anything, it would have been a confrontation," I shrugged.

"Only if you made it a confrontation. Look," Auntie Jill said, taking my hand and leading me to a bench out by the front of the museum. "I'm not telling you to get in the girl's face or start yelling — that's not what I'm talking about. But Mina, you do need to start sticking up for yourself. You take all that criticism and backtalk from Paulette in class and get upset about it but you bite your tongue instead of defending yourself. And even when you're just hanging out with friends, you tend to run off when you don't succeed right away."

I hadn't known she'd seen the whole Double Dutch episode.

"Uh-huh, I saw it," Auntie said as if she were reading my mind. "The minute someone challenges you or pushes you or tells you they want more, you shrink back or walk away. I can tell you personally that that's not the way of Chestnut women."

I smiled a little at Auntie's words; it was nice to be thought of as a Chestnut woman.

"But — how do I *do* it exactly?" I asked.

"Well, in the case of what happened with Paulette, as soon as she started taking credit for the project you guys did together, you could have added your own comments to the mix. I'm not saying you should have yelled out, 'She's lying! I'm the one who came up with the idea!' But you could have said something like, 'I'm glad you like our project, Ms. Roberts. I actually came up with this idea, but Paulette was helpful in such and such way.' And today, when those girls were laughing at your jump rope mishap, you could have simply gotten up, shaken it off, and tried again."

"Easier said than done," I grumbled, but I knew that my aunt had a point.

"Look, Mina, all I'm saying is that you weren't raised to be this shy girl playing in the background while everyone else steals your shine. You're a terrific little artist and you're only going to get better. But you have to find your voice. Speak up, baby, and you'll be heard," she continued, patting my hand. "Now, I have to go into my meeting. It won't take long. You going to be okay out here?"

"Yes," I said, forcing a smile to my face.

"It's going to be all right, sweetie. Why don't you go into the gift shop and see if there's anything in there you like. I think they have some Bearden postcards in there."

"Okay, Auntie," I said as I stood up from the bench.

She was right; there were plenty of Bearden postcards, and books about him, too. I flipped through a couple of them, feeling my spirits lift, and then sauntered over to a table with a bunch of colorful jewelry on it.

"Those bracelets are from Kenya," a woman standing near the register called out. "Some of them are made with leather, and some have cowrie shells attached to them. They're made by people in the villages there, and no two bracelets are ever alike."

I leaned in a little closer to the bracelets. "They're beautiful," I said, smiling genuinely for the first time in quite a while. I ran my fingers across the beads of a black-and-green bracelet; the beads were arranged in a way that made the green beads look like arrowheads pointing in the same direction all the way around the bracelet.

"Green and black are my best friend's favorite colors," I said, trying the bracelet on my arm. It was a perfect fit, which meant it'd probably fit on Liza's arm, too, seeing as we're practically the same size. I was thinking she'd dig the bracelet, too, because it was so different from anything she'd probably have ever seen. And how cool was it that someone actually strung all those beads on the leather?

"How much is it?" I asked, pulling it off my arm.

"It's twenty-five dollars, and all the proceeds go directly to the collective of Kenyan artists who made it, so you'll be giving both yourself and the artists a great gift!" she exclaimed.

"Yeah, this would make a great gift, wouldn't it?" I said, handing the bracelet to her. "I'll take it."

"Great, I'll wrap it up for you. Come on to the register and I'll ring you up," she said.

"Um, I kinda have to wait for my aunt. She's in a meeting, and she's also the one with the money, so . . ."

"Oh," the lady laughed. "I understand. I'll just leave it over here and when your aunt comes in, we'll settle up, okay?"

"Okay," I said.

"Did you enjoy the art exhibit?" she asked as she removed the tag from the bracelet and wrapped it in tissue paper.

"Well, I only got a quick look at it."

"You have some time on your hands — go back in there and enjoy the art," she said. "You won't find anything like it in too many museums. You're here; you might as well take a look, right?"

"You're right. I think I will," I said, bounding out of the gift shop and into the gallery.

The art was looking much brighter.

Chapter Eight

Uptown — that's what Auntie Jill calls Harlem — was crazy! In a good way. After her meeting at the museum, Auntie took me on a walking tour of the neighborhood to see all these brownstones and restaurants and big, beautiful churches, and places where people were showing off their talent. Auntie gave me a dollar to toss into the hat of a trumpet player who was playing a slow, melodic version of "Amazing Grace," the way you hear it in church early Sunday morning. He smiled and nodded a thank-you, never once taking his lips off his horn. Just around the corner was the Schomburg Center, a huge library full of books and art produced by black people from all across the world.

“You know, when I was a college student at Columbia University, I used to come here and look through the stacks and stacks of books and papers they have here,” Auntie said as we walked through the halls of the library. The museumlike displays chronicled the history of black people in America.

When we left the library, she walked me past the stately cottages that lined what she called Strivers’ Row, a neighborhood where rich black actors and politicians used to live. Auntie showed me the houses where the poet Langston Hughes and Madam C. J. Walker, the richest black woman in the world (before Oprah even!) used to live.

“And here is where I saw my first live concert,” Auntie said, pointing up at the marquee of the Apollo, where some of the world’s most famous singers and dancers used to give concerts. “New Edition was performing. I just loved them, but boy, was it a rowdy affair when the amateur contest started. The audience didn’t have a problem cheering on the good singers, but when they didn’t like a performer, they booed and booed. I felt sorry for whoever was on the receiving end of that super-loud crowd.”

I nodded, thinking about how hard it was to get rejection, to hear criticism.

"But you know what?" Auntie said, watching me closely. "Those singers kept on going, kept on trying, despite all the boos. I was amazed by them!" I smiled at my auntie, realizing she'd told me the story for a reason. After all, if the people trying out at the Apollo could stand tall, I could survive art camp. I reached out and squeezed her hand.

Later, we stopped for lunch at a restaurant called Miss Mamie's Spoonbread, Too, and even the food tasted better in Harlem. The fried fish, collard greens, and candied sweet potatoes were super-tasty and reminded me of my mom's cooking. It was definitely a nice break from Auntie's tofu and beans and fruit dip. Anyway, Auntie really showed me some cool stuff in Harlem — enough to make me think that it might be a neat place to live when I get old enough to go to college and live on my own. Well, after I live in a fab apartment in Fort Greene, and maybe spend a year or two in SoHo.

I'd never felt the urge to draw something the way I did when Auntie and I got back to her place. No doubt, I was on a mission: I had decided to make a story quilt. It would show pictures of city buildings and sidewalks and stoops, and people with broad noses and large brown eyes and colorful hats, just like the beautiful sights, sounds, and people I'd seen during our walk.

"Mina!" Auntie Jill yelled as she walked into my room/our art studio to find me tearing through her latest issue of *Essence*. A pile of other magazines and massive amounts of cutout pictures and scraps were spread out all over the floor. "Tell me you didn't cut up all my magazines!"

"I, um, I . . ." I began, looking down at my handiwork. "It's for a project I'm making."

Auntie narrowed her eyes and put her hands on her hips. "But those are my good magazines," she said, bending over to pick up the magazine I was in the middle of cutting to shreds. "I still had some things in here I wanted to read."

"Sorry, Auntie," I said genuinely. "I guess I should have asked. It's just that I wanted to make a story quilt about Harlem, and these have the best pictures."

Auntie Jill flipped through a few more pages in the magazine and then handed it back to me. "Girl, that picture you're making better be better than a Bearden and worth all my good magazines having to go in the recycling bin, I'll tell you that much. Just don't tear out the page with the sandals on it — I saw something cute in there I think I might want.

"And speaking of cute," she continued, "I need you to pick out something special to wear because I'm taking you to a beach party tonight."

My eyes grew wide as saucers as I hopped to my feet and did a happy dance. "Are you serious? We're going to the beach? Omigosh, I can't breathe. I miss the beach so much and you're taking me? I have to get my bathing suit, and do you have a big beach towel I can borrow because I didn't bring my favorite purple one because I didn't think we'd ever make it to the beach," I said as I rushed over to my bureau and started tossing my clothes in search of my cute purple-striped bikini. "Are we going to Jones Beach out on Long Island? I mean, it *is* famous and all. . . ."

"Whoa, whoa — easy!" Auntie Jill laughed. "We're not going to Jones Beach."

"Oh," I said, a little confused. What other beach was there in New York? I thought on it a sec. "Oh!" I exclaimed. "We're going to Coney Island! Do you think we can ride on the Ferris wheel before we go suntanning and . . ."

"We're not going to Coney Island either," she laughed.

"Really? What, are we driving to the Jersey shore?"

"No," Auntie Jill said, picking up the clothes I tossed on the floor and neatly folding them. "We're going to tar beach."

"Where's that? Connecticut?" I asked innocently.

That time, Auntie Jill let out a deep, loud laugh. "No, girl! Tar beach isn't in Connecticut! It's right here in Brooklyn, right here in this brownstone."

I wrinkled my brow and gave Auntie the eye. "I don't get it," I finally said. "Here?"

"Yes, here," she said, trying to contain her giggles. "Baby, tar beach isn't exactly a beach like the ones you go to in New Jersey. It's the rooftop of a city building. It's called a beach because that's where people who live in the city go to lie out and relax, just like you do on the beach, and the tar part refers to the tar material that the roof is usually made of."

"Oh," I said, feeling silly. "A tar beach party. So, um, I guess I won't be needing this," I said, holding up my bathing suit.

"Yeah — no bathing suit necessary," she said. "Just put on something cute. I'm inviting a few friends over and we're going to have some appetizers and snacks and drinks and a little music — nothing big."

"Cool," I said, excited by the idea. "Hey — can I invite Gabriella?"

"Sure," Auntie said. "She's a sweet girl. I'm glad you two made friends."

"Yeah, me too," I answered. "She turned out to be way cooler than I thought she'd be. Almost as cool as Sam and Liza."

"Well, that's certainly a huge compliment coming from you. I know how you feel about your Sam and Liza," Auntie said, smiling.

"Yeah," I said, sneaking a glance at the framed picture of me and my girls.

"Well, Gabriella can come over tonight if her mom says it's okay for her to come. The party doesn't start until seven thirty, so maybe she can come earlier and help us set up, and then we can both walk her back home when the party's over. Give me her number and I'll call her mom to get permission and everything."

"Alrighty, then — a party on tar beach," I said as I sat back on the floor and picked up my scissors to resume destroying Auntie's magazines. Auntie took one final look at the mess and smiled.

"Okay, and baby? You're going to clean all that up before company comes, clear?"

"Clear," I said.

Gabriella set the tray of raw broccoli, carrots, and dip on a small, candlelit table and then spread out a small stack of napkins next to the tray. "Yum. Broccoli," she said, wrinkling her nose.

"You think that's bad, you should taste the fried bean balls she made with the yogurt dip," I whispered, looking around to see if my aunt was within earshot. She wasn't. But the roof was slowly filling with a bunch of Auntie's friends, each of them more fabulous than the last. There were artists and poets, writers, and even musicians who showed up with instruments. One guy, whose locs swung just past the backs of his knees, even pulled out his bongos and beat out an African rhythm that drew a crowd of onlookers, some who sang a song while he drummed, others who broke out into dance.

Auntie was over near the action, clapping and laughing and offering glasses of fresh fruit punch to the guests. The air was electric — the crowd was taking on a colorful life of its own as their bodies swayed against the backdrop of sparkling city lights.

"I did convince my aunt to get some other food besides fried bean balls and broccoli," I added. "I can fix you a sandwich or something. I think there's some sliced turkey and cheese in the fridge downstairs."

"Eh, I'm not really hungry. My mom made arroz con pollo. I'm stuffed."

"A rose?"

"No, silly, arroz con pollo," she said, pronouncing each word slowly. "It means rice and chicken in Spanish."

"Ah, gotcha. I wouldn't have minded a plate of that," I laughed.

"There were some leftovers. I can totally go get you a plate," Gabriella offered.

"Nah, it's cool. I'm not that hungry. But thanks for offering."

"No sweat," Gabriella said easily, walking over to the wall of the roof. I followed her and settled into a spot right next to her.

"You know, I think I owe you an apology for what happened earlier today," she said, staring out over the houses that stood at attention on Auntie's block. "When we were playing Double Dutch? KeKe didn't mean anything by what she said. . . ."

"I know," I said, cutting off Gabriella. "No need to apologize. I was being extra sensitive for no reason. It's totally cool."

Gabriella made a sound like she was holding her breath and then letting it out. "Thank goodness," she said. "I really thought you were mad at me. I was so happy when your aunt called to invite me over."

"Nah, I wasn't mad," I insisted. "I just had a few things on my mind, that's all. And, well, like I said, I'd never jumped double Dutch before. I guess I was a little embarrassed by that."

Gabriella nodded. "I could try teaching you again, if you want," she volunteered. "Just the two of us this time."

"I'd like that," I said gratefully.

Gabriella and I sat staring out over the city.

"I love tar beach parties," she said. "My *abuelita* used to have them all the time. She'd invite the neighbors and they'd play cards and checkers and Pokeno and dance and laugh. It was always so much fun." Gabriella stopped herself and got quiet. "My grandmother died last year."

"Wow," I said, hesitating, not sure what to say.

"Yeah, I miss her a lot."

"I once had a cat that died," I said, and then

groaned, instantly feeling a little dumb for saying that. Did I really just compare the death of my cat to her grandmother's? "I mean, of course, that's not as serious as your grandmother's death, but . . ."

"Oh, it's okay," Gabriella said, putting her arm across my shoulder. "I understand where you're coming from. It's cool."

We both fell silent, staring out over the rooftop as the drummer continued to bang his beat and the laughter of the guests pierced the air.

"You know," I said, "if you squint your eyes while you stare at the buildings across Brooklyn, the lights look like diamonds and stars."

We both tried it, squinting first at the buildings and then at each other — looking like two crazy girls with eyesight problems. We giggled again.

"Do you think you'd like to live in Brooklyn one day?" Gabriella asked.

"Maybe. It's where artists live, and I want to be an artist, just like my aunt. She's got a pretty neat life. I mean, look at her friends. Can you get any cooler than this? It sure ain't Greenwood."

"I love Brooklyn, but I don't want to stay here forever. When I look out at the buildings, I wonder what's out past them, you know? The sky looks so big. I think the world must be as big as the sky. I want to see the world," Gabriella sighed.

"So you don't want to be an artist?" I asked.

"Oh, I do. But I think it would be kinda the bomb to be an artist in Paris. Or in Italy, where you could paint a field of flowers in Tuscany. Or even go to where my mom grew up in the Dominican Republic and see what life is like there."

"Hey, Gabriella? I'm really glad I met you," I said easily. And I was.

"Same here," Gabriella said. "At first, I thought you didn't really like me. But I knew you'd come around. Most people can't resist my charms," she said, putting her hands on her hips and striking a pose.

"Oh, whatever!" I said, striking an identical pose. "Seriously, though: I didn't mean to come off so quiet at first. I'm just not used to being around this many people. New York City can be . . . tough."

"It can." Gabriella nodded. "It's an insane place, and it's hard to keep up with the pace. But I actually think you're doing a great job."

"Thanks," I said with a smile.

The two of us stared out over the city a little while longer and then turned around to survey

Auntie's tar beach party. It had gotten so crowded that it was hard for people to dance to the drummer's beat, so he stopped drumming and grabbed himself a root beer. I saw Auntie flipping through her iPod and then standing it on her portable speaker system; seconds later, the air was filled with soft soul music. She smiled and moved through the crowd, talking to each of her guests like every one of them was her best friend.

"Man, when I grow up, I'm gonna try to be like your auntie," Gabriella said, mesmerized.

"Me too." I smiled, bending over the table to swirl a piece of broccoli in the vegetable dip. I took a small bite and winced a little. "Except I'm totally going to serve chicken wings and pigs in blankets at my parties!"

"I know that's right!" Gabriella said, extending her hand for a high five.

Our hands connected and slapped together like fireworks in the warm, night sky.

Chapter Nine

"But I thought you loved the red velvet cupcakes," Auntie said as she expertly dodged a rush of people making their way down the subway stairs as we made our way up.

We were just back from a grueling day at art camp; Ms. Roberts had us running all around Central Park sketching animals. This time, I'd been paired with Lee Woo. He was a nice enough guy, but he's allergic to grass and on that particular morning, he forgot to take his medicine, which meant he spent way more time sneezing on me and my sketches than he did actually getting his work done. And it seemed that every time I tried to move away from him, he'd move that much closer to me.

But ducking and dodging his sneezes had been worth it; I got to see the biggest, most beautiful park ever. The green of the grass stretched as far as my eyes could see, all of it surrounded by trees whose leaves flitted in the wind, making music with the birds who chirped and danced on their branches. There were buildings standing sentry over the treetops, and kids pranced and skipped through Sheep Meadow.

Of course, Lee had to be a boy about it. "I really, really, really want to go see the polar bears in the Central Park Zoo," he told me and our assigned Central Park tour guide, "and my mom told me a long time ago that . . ." A sneeze seized his words; he wiped his nose on his shoulder.

"Bless you," I said, wrinkling my nose. Hey, I couldn't pretend anymore like his constant sneezing and wheezing wasn't gross. I did kinda feel sorry for him, though.

"My mom told me that there's a polar bear who's depressed and needs pills to feel good about himself."

"Oh, stop it!" I said, folding my arms. "A depressed polar bear?" I glanced at our tour guide, who only shrugged.

"I'm new," he told us.

“We should go see it,” Lee said, marching off in the direction of the zoo. “We can draw the polar bear. It’ll be the perfect New York scene.”

“Um, hold on there, buddy — there’s just one problem,” I said, looking in the park map Ms. Roberts had given us. “I don’t want to draw the polar bear, and besides, you need money to get into the zoo,” I added, pointing at the fee schedule in the guide. “Unless, of course, you have twenty dollars to pay to get us in.”

Silence.

“Right, okay. So no polar bears for us. But since we need to draw animals, how about we head over to the Central Park Carousel,” I said, tapping the picture on the map. “It’s free, and you can draw a horse and a crazy kid riding it. I mean, it’s not a depressed polar bear, but it could be pretty cool and colorful, right?”

Lee sneezed and wiped.

“Alrighty then,” I said.

“It’s just this way,” our guide told us, leading us to the carousel.

An hour and a half later, I was standing next to Gabriella. And as far away from Sneezy as I could get.

“Honest to goodness, I think there’s more of

Lee's snot on my pictures than paint," I told Gabriella as we sat waiting for Ms. Roberts to critique our work. Gabriella covered her mouth to hide her giggle.

Ms. Roberts praised Paulette's painting of a red-breasted robin bouncing around a nest, and Paulette beamed like the painting was good enough for the Metropolitan Museum of Art. All I got was the "good work, Mina" when Ms. Roberts looked at my painting of the carousel horses.

"Um, Mina? Are you even listening to me?" Auntie Jill asked, snapping her fingers in my direction to get my attention.

"I'm listening," I said, giving her a half smile.

"Before you know it, you won't be able to go over to The Spot anymore, seeing as you'll be going back home in a week," Auntie continued, navigating down Fulton Street, with Gabriella and me close on her heels.

"Yeah," Gabriella chimed in. "One more week and no more red velvet cupcakes. Will you ever forgive yourself if you don't go?"

I shook my head. It had been a long day, and I was tired as all get-out and plus I really didn't want to run into Marley, especially with Gabriella in tow, seeing as she was dead set on setting us up.

"You know, Auntie Jill, you're contributing to my habit," I insisted, giggling. "Any other day, you'd be telling me to skip the sweets and eat a big plate of your baked tofu and gravy," I added, playfully wrinkling my nose.

"Uh-huh. Well, Auntie has needs, and I need to get back to the house for my phone conference and I also need a red velvet cupcake. So I'm asking my darling niece to be a dear and go to a restaurant right around the corner from the house and pick me up a cupcake. Is that too much to ask for your auntie, who's fed you and given you shelter and an easel of your own these last two months? Is it?" Auntie asked breathlessly.

"Plus, it's Poetry Slam Wednesday," Gabriella chimed in. And then, under her breath she added, "Marley's going to be there."

I gave Gabriella the evil eye.

"Right, it's Wednesday," Auntie said. "You can go and get in a little bit of poetry, check out some art, and grab me a red velvet or two to go."

"Yeah, I can even come with you if Ms. Jill calls my mom. She won't mind if I go, so long as I tell her where I'm going," Gabriella said.

"Well, it's all settled, then," Auntie said, pulling out her cell and pushing the speed-dial button for Gabriella's house. "Be a dear and bring back two cupcakes for me, will you?" she said as she turned down South Elliott Place and made a beeline for her brownstone stoop. "Oh, and use the change from the twenty I gave you for lunch!"

I stopped at the corner, my left arm aching from carrying my super-stuffed art case. I rolled my eyes at Gabriella. "Thanks a lot," I said.

"What?" Gabriella asked innocently.

"You just contributed to the madness," I said, shaking my head. "You couldn't just help me out and go back to the house, huh? Say something about how all those calories and red dye in the cupcakes is unhealthy or something, huh?"

"Come on," Gabriella said, pulling my arm just as the light turned green. "It'll be fun."

"I'll go, but you have to promise me you won't say anything to Marley about me," I insisted.

"My lips are sealed," Gabriella said.

I hated to admit it, but Gabriella was right about The Spot. We walked in just in time to see Darwin, a local performer who had had a guest appearance as an extra on *iCarly*, strumming his guitar and singing a song about rain. The entire café was on its feet, clapping to his music and dancing in the tiny spaces between the tables. Gabriella and I scanned for an empty table, but there were none. Marley was there, though—standing over by the diner counter, sipping on a Sprite and nodding his head to the beat. The sight of him made my heart jump.

"Oh, well. Looks like there aren't any more seats. We should probably get the cupcakes to go, then," I said, turning to head toward the cupcake display.

Gabriella paid me no mind; she waved at a table full of friends and headed in their direction. "Come on, they won't mind if we sit with them," she said, taking off before I could protest.

Reluctantly, I followed along.

Gabriella exchanged hugs with all three girls at the table, and yelled out, "Everybody, this is Mina. Mina? This is everybody. I'll tell you everybody's names when Darwin stops singing," she said, dropping her art case on the floor and joining in on the clapping.

"It's nice to meet you all." I smiled warmly. "Um, I'm going to go over and get those cupcakes before they're all sold out. If I go back to Auntie's without them, she might make me sleep on the front stoop," I said, leaning into Gabriella's ear so she could hear me.

"Okay, cool," she said. "We'll be right here. Leave your art bag—I'll watch it," she added.

I handed her my art supplies and made a beeline for the counter, alternately squeezing between people and saying "excuse me" as I pushed through the crowd. I felt like I'd just run a football gauntlet by the time I got there, and I was sweaty. The air conditioner was working overtime against the ninety-degree heat outside, but The Spot was so thick with bodies that the air coming out of the vents felt more like a small breeze than cool, comforting air. I reached into my pocket and pulled out a purple handkerchief and tied it around my locs.

"I'll have four red velvet cupcakes," I told the guy behind the counter.

"Coming up," he said.

"That's a lot of cupcakes for one person. You sharing?" I heard a voice say.

I turned and jumped when I realized who was talking. It was Marley.

"I, um, I'm kinda getting a couple to go," I stuttered, turning back to the register guy. "Um, can I get three of those in a to-go box? Thanks."

"Right. I'll take a cupcake, too," Marley told the counter guy. "Just one for me."

I looked up at him and smiled uncomfortably, then turned back toward the counter and stared at the cupcakes, too nervous to say much of anything else.

"So, you enjoying yourself?" he asked.

"We just got here," I said. "Gabriella and I, I mean."

"Oh, Gabby's here? Cool," he said, nodding.

"Yeah, um, cool. I mean, um, she's cool."

"Yeah," he said easily. "So, when am I going to see you take the mike?"

"Uh, never!" I said, shaking my head.

"Why not?" Marley asked. "What, you don't have any talents? You must have something in that big ol' art-supplies box."

He noticed my art-supplies box. Omigod.

"Just some paint and brushes," I said.

"So you and Gabriella paint, huh? Nice," he said, nodding.

"Thanks," I said.

"So that's a talent," he added. "You can paint."

"Yeah, but I don't play the guitar or do poetry like you, so . . ."

"Ah, but you draw. You should come up with me on the stage and paint while I kick a verse," he said, taking his cupcake from the counter guy.

"Uh, no — no thanks," I said. "I'm going to go

ahead and eat my cupcake and leave the stage to the performers."

"Come on — what are you, scared?"

Just then, Gabriella bounced up to us and threw her arm around my shoulders. "What's up, Marley?" she said breezily. And then, to me: "You leave us any red velvets?"

"There are plenty left," I laughed.

"What's up, Gabby?" Marley said. "I was just trying to talk your girl here into coming up on the stage with me and drawing while I knock out a quick verse."

"You should totally do it!" Gabriella exclaimed.

"Uh, no, I'm going to eat my cupcake and . . ." I began, but Gabriella was having none of that.

"Come on, you can totally do it!" she said, cutting me off. "What's the poem about?" she asked Marley.

"It's called 'Harlem,'" he said simply.

"See? You've been working on story quilts about Harlem at home, Mina. It's perfect!" Gabriella exclaimed.

"I don't think —"

"Come on — you have your art-supplies box right over there, and I'm sure the manager wouldn't mind lending you a piece of paper or a tablecloth or something. Oh man, this is going to be incredible. Let's get your stuff," Gabriella said, grabbing my hand.

"Hold on to these cupcakes, would you?" Marley said to the counter guy as Gabriella dragged me over to our table. I barely got a chance to protest before she swooped up my art-supplies box and dragged me over to the stage.

"And next up," the DJ shouted into the mike, "is a crowd favorite, and he's brought along a newbie to the stage to draw while he kicks a verse. Please give a hand to Marley and Mina!"

The crowd, still hyped from the last performer, clapped wildly for me and Marley. He grabbed my art box from Gabriella with one hand, took my hand with the other, and practically pulled me up to the stage. Gabriella grabbed the piece of white butcher paper covering our table, brought it up to the stage, and set it up on the easel. I slowly took my art box from Marley's hands and tried not to faint. My hands were trembling. But when I looked over at Gabriella, she was smiling — which put me at ease, if only a little.

"Why don't you do it with me?" I said to Gabriella as I hurriedly squeezed out paints onto the palette.

"No, girl, you got this!" Gabriella said, shaking her head violently. "Go for it."

"Hold up, wait — *you're* scared?" I asked, smiling in wonder.

"I'm not scared," Gabriella said, nervously surveying the crowd. "It's just that Marley asked you."

"Whatev, you're totally his friend — he won't care," I insisted. "Plus, it's your fault I'm up here, anyway. I'll sketch; you paint."

Just as I squeezed the last of the paint onto the palette, Marley loosened the mike from its stand and looked over at Gabriella and me. "She's helping," I mouthed confidently with a smile.

Marley smiled back and nodded. "Cool," he mouthed back. Then, into the mike, he said, "This poem is called 'Harlem.' I know Mina and Gabriella are going to do something dope."

When the audience applause finally quieted down, the DJ mixed a beat as Marley leaned into the mike and spun a fantastic rhyme about city buildings, street corner vendors, and streets paved with gold — uptown roots, Double Dutching, Strivers' Row, and the Apollo. Every word he said inspired my pastels to fly across the butcher paper: Brownstones materialized, then a steep stoop, and a lady with a big textured Afro, watching her kids play Double Dutch. I couldn't believe how fast my hands were moving, creating a scene painted by Marley's words. Gabriella was keeping up, too, adding bold colors to my sketch that made the pictures pop off the page.

When Marley finished up his rhyme, Gabriella and I stood back from our painting. It wasn't finished — the little girls' clothes weren't colored in, and the windows in a couple of the brownstones were missing, and the sky was only half painted blue, but it totally looked like the streets Auntie and I had explored just the other day, when she was encouraging me to stick up for myself and acknowledge that for a twelve-year-old, I painted pretty good.

"Everybody, show your love for Marley!" the DJ called out as our friend pumped his fist in the air and grinned at the wild applause. Marley's grin grew even wider when he strutted over to the easel and saw the picture Gabriella and I created.

"Man! That's amazing!" he said, standing back to admire the painting. "I can't believe you guys just did that."

I couldn't contain my excitement — I had to admit the picture was kinda awesome.

"You gotta sign it," Marley said as the DJ called out over the mike for us to show the audience our painting. "You gotta write the word *Harlem* on that. That painting is bananas."

Gabriella hurriedly signed her name in hot-pink pastel; I used purple and added a swirl at the top of the *I* in my name, which I wrote in all capital letters; then I scribbled *Harlem* beneath it. And, together, Gabriella and I grabbed the sides of the easel and turned our painting around so that our audience could see it.

The hooting and hollering and hand claps were deafening!

I looked at Gabriella and she looked at me and we broke out into hysterics and high-fived each other like we'd just won the Super Bowl. Marley joined in and put his arms around both of our shoulders, which, of course, made Gabriella and I look at each other and laugh even harder.

I was totally thinking, *Thank goodness for red velvet cupcakes and Harlem!*

Seriously, if I could have bottled my happy juice right then? All of Brooklyn would have been floating — that's how happy I was. I mean, that hour and a half totally ranked right up there with the time I won the math team competition against Tye Lawrence in our gifted class (after he told everybody the entire two weeks leading up to our math showdown that he was smarter than me), and definitely the time when Sam set me up with the winning shot in our big summer soccer tournament. Even though I got trophies from both the math competition and the soccer tournament, I won much more doing that performance art: I got my confidence back.

My only wish was that Liza and Samantha had been there to see it. Gabriella was a welcome stand-in, though.

"How cool is it that they're going to hang our picture up in The Spot?" Gabriella said as we practically skipped down Fulton, our art cases and bags of red velvet cupcakes dangling from our hands.

"Where do you think they'll put it?" I asked, peeking into storefront windows as we walked.

"I don't know." Gabriella shrugged. "If it's not behind the cupcake counter next to the red velvet display, I'm writing a letter to the president!"

"Wow," I laughed. "So what are you trying to say?"

"It could be a tribute to your addiction," she said. "They could put a plaque under it that says: *'Here lies a tribute to the red velvet cake bandit. Guard your velvet!'*"

I was still giggling over that one when we passed Sheets, a music store tucked between an African clothing store and a small Jamaican restaurant. In the window, there was a collection of songbooks and sheet music, one of which caught my attention: It was a song called "Under the Boardwalk." I stopped so short that Gabriella ran into my back.

"Dude!"

"Wait — oh, I'm sorry," I laughed. "Check it out — it's sheet music."

"Okaaay," Gabriella said, confused.

"No, it's just that my friend Samantha just started teaching herself how to play guitar," I said.

"And . . ." Gabriella said, trying to hurry my point.

"Well, I want to send her something, like a souvenir from my trip to Brooklyn, and I've been trying to think of something super-awesome to get her and I think I just found it," I said, walking into the store.

Gabriella shrugged and followed me inside.

"Excuse me," I called out to a little old lady sitting behind the register. "How much is that sheet music in the window — the 'Under the Boardwalk' music?"

The old lady pushed herself up off her roller chair and creaked over to the window. "Oh, this one?" she asked, picking it up. "That's a great song. You're a fan of the Drifters, are you?"

"Well, I've never heard the song," I offered. "But it says 'Under the Boardwalk.' That's where my best friends and I used to hang out when we were little kids and we played together on the Jersey Shore."

"That sounds like a lot of fun," the lady said.

"It was." I smiled easily. "How much did you say it costs?"

"That'll be four dollars," she said.

I reached into my pocket and pulled out two crinkled dollar bills and seventy-two cents in change. "I don't have enough," I said sadly.

"Well, yeah, you spent almost all your money on cupcakes," Gabriella laughed as she reached into her pocket. She pulled out a neatly folded five-dollar bill. "This oughta do it."

"Thanks," I said. "I appreciate that. I'll pay you back tomorrow. I really want to take this music home now so I can put a little paint on it."

"Paint?" the old lady asked as she took Gabriella's five-dollar bill and rang up the price on the register.

"Yeah," I said. "My friend Sam and I love the beach. It would look pretty cool if I paint a picture of the boardwalk and the beach on it."

"Nice," Gabriella said as she watched the lady put the sheet music in a paper protector and slip it into a bag. "You know, you never talked about your friends from back home. I was starting to think you didn't have any."

"I never told you about Samantha and Liza?" I asked.

"Nope," Gabriella said. "But I'm sure they're cool."

"Definitely," I said, smiling. There wasn't any need to say another word. We just beamed all the way down Fulton Street, until she went her way and I went mine.

When I got back to Auntie's apartment, I dropped off her cupcakes and then went straight up to my room and right up to the chalkboard wall. With a yellow chalk, I wrote the word *happy* in big bubble letters, and then colored them in with bright pink polka-dot smiley faces.

My board was bright, but not nearly as bright as I was feeling right then.

Chapter Ten

"Wait. I need one more piece of the gold material, and then I'm done," I said, rummaging through a huge pile of scrap fabric, torn pieces of paper, beads, buttons, ribbon, and fancy stationery. Auntie Jill had given me all the goods after a little begging and pleading on my part.

"But baby, if you keep piling stuff onto your picture, it's not going to have enough time to dry before you have to present it to the judges," Auntie said. "This has to be the last piece, sweetie pie."

I pulled a tiny piece of gold-leaf paper out from the pile. I applied glue from the hot glue gun onto the edges, then carefully pasted the paper to the canvas on my easel. It was my final art project, the one that was supposed to represent everything I'd learned over the summer.

"There," I said, standing back to admire my picture.

"Oh! That sure is a fine piece of work," a voice called out from behind us.

It was Mom! I screamed and laughed and ran into her arms.

"I didn't hear you guys come in," I said, squeezing her waist and snuggling into her. "I've missed you!"

"We've missed you, too, pumpkin," my dad said, walking into the room with two overnight bags. My sister followed behind him, with a big box in her hands. She tossed me a half smile, which, clearly, was about as welcoming as she was going to get, even though we hadn't seen each other in six whole weeks. But whatev.

"Daddy!" I squealed, loosening my grip on my mom so that I could pull him into a group hug. "Omigosh, I can't believe you guys are here!"

"Live and in the flesh," Daddy said. "Did you have a good time, sweetheart?"

"Did Auntie Jill take good care of you?" my mom chimed in, without giving me a chance to answer the first question.

"So are you going to be a vegetarian and eat

tofu and broccoli all the time?" my sister asked, leaning against the door.

"Whoa, whoa, whoa!" Auntie laughed. "She had a great time because she was with me, and of course I took great care of my niece. And as for you, Miss Lady, I'll have you know that tofu and broccoli is not only good for you; it's quite delicious."

"Uh, yeah, okay," my dad laughed, hugging his sister. "I'm sure we could stand here and debate the merits of eliminating an entire food group from our diets, but don't we have to get going?" he asked, looking at his watch. "We have about an hour until the show starts, and the traffic over the Brooklyn Bridge is getting kinda ugly. We should get a move on."

"Oh, goodness, we sure should. I don't want my baby missing out on her big win!" Mom exclaimed.

"Aw, Mom, I don't know if you should be claiming the top prize for me just yet," I said. "A lot of the kids in the program are really good."

"As good as this?" she asked, walking over to the artwork I had just finished. "Mina, this is absolutely beautiful!"

"Thanks, Mom," I said, smiling. "But you're kinda supposed to say that."

"Mina! I'm not just saying it because you're my daughter, trust," she said. "You know I'd tell you if it wasn't just right. Your painting is really great. Now hurry up and get changed," my mom said, clapping her hands. "Let's go, baby, or we're going to be late."

"Mom, I'm not getting changed — I'm wearing this," I said, looking down at my oversize purple hooded dress and pink polka-dotted leggings. Earlier, Auntie Jill pulled my locs into two low ponytails, and let me use a little of her lip gloss, even though my mom doesn't really like me wearing makeup. Shoot, I looked cute!

"Mina, you're wearing sneakers," my mom said, wrinkling her nose and looking at me disapprovingly.

"Oh, girl, we've been through this already," Auntie Jill said. "She's got to wear the lucky Converses because Sam and Liza signed them for good luck, and if she doesn't, she greatly reduces her chances of winning — blah blah blah."

My mom shook her head and gave my Converses the stare down.

"Speaking of Liza," my little sister said, "you got something in the mail." She shoved the padded envelope she'd been carrying in my direction.

"What is it?" I asked.

"Well, if you read the label, you'd see it's something from Liza," my sister snapped.

"Liza!" I exclaimed, grabbing the package from my sister's hands. A wild giggle made its way into my throat.

I sat on my daybed and ripped open the envelope, pulling off layers of tissues to get to the Liza goodness.

"What's that?" my mom asked as I pulled out a photograph of Liza balancing on the top of a fence, soaking wet with her arms raised triumphantly in the air. And under layers of wrapping paper was, of all things, a small cowboy lizard figurine.

"Omigod, Liza is such a nut!" I laughed as I flipped over the photo. On the back, in her trademark bubble letters, Liza had written, *Wish You Were Here! Love, Lizard.*

Lizard? Was that her new nickname? Did it have something to do with the lizard cowboy? I couldn't help cracking up. The funny photo and the random figurine were just so . . . Liza.

She never had a problem being exactly who she was, and she never seemed pressed to be anything else. And if she wanted to climb a fence, or decide to go by Lizard for the summer, then that's what she was going to do, no matter what anybody else had to say about it. I loved that about her.

It was inspiring.

"What's up, sweetie?" Auntie asked, picking up the picture to give it a once-over. "These are really cute gifts. Is this Liza?"

"Yes." I nodded, a smile crossing my face from ear to ear, even as tears filled my eyes.

"She's quite the character," Auntie said, picking up the figurine.

"Uh-huh," I pushed out.

"Well, it sure was thoughtful of her to send you these. You should make sure you say thank you properly, okay? Maybe you can send her a thank-you note."

"Well, um," I said, clearing my throat and fighting back the tears, "she's on vacation with her family and I don't know how long she'll be at the address on the envelope."

"Hmm, well, maybe you can send it to her house so it'll be waiting for her when she gets back," my dad said.

"That's a good idea," I said, my heart warming at the thought. "But maybe I'll send her an e-mail instead. Even if she isn't able to check it until she gets back. I'll do it right now."

My dad looked at his watch and shook his head no. "We have to leave, baby," he insisted.

"Daddy, it'll take only a minute," I said, running down the stairs and toward Auntie's laptop. "I promise!"

I found Auntie's laptop on the small kitchen table; thankfully, it was already on and set to go. I logged in to my e-mail account and typed in Liza's e-mail addy.

Lizard! ☺

Thanks for the super-cutie gifts! What's up with that wacky photo? Um, not for nothing, but who dared you to do that? I hope you're still collecting allowance while you're out on the road; you're going to need some hush money to keep me from making copies and posting it on the bulletin board at school — LOL! I really like the cowboy lizard, too. Where'd you get it from? Are you having fun wherever you are? And where exactly are you, anyway?

I just wanted to say thanks — and not just for the gifts. But for helping me walk into my art competition with confidence. I'll explain more when we see each other again, but let's just say your cowboy is going to help me rope my prize.

You so rock.

Miss you,

Mina

"All right, sweet potato, it's time to blow this taco stand," my dad called out as he made his way down the stairs, my artwork in tow. "Let's boogie."

"Let's," I said, shutting down the computer.

It was showtime.

"Hmm, the sheet does wonders for her art, doesn't it?" Paulette said, smiling sweetly as she, Stephanie, and Mariska filed past my painting. It'd just been hung on the wall and, like all the other art in the final show, would remain covered until the judges' big reveal.

Gabriella set the record straight. "Dude, don't pay her any attention," she said, wringing her hands and pacing back and forth. She gave a nervous wave to her mom, who was sitting with my parents and all of the other family members of my fellow campers. The spectator section.

"Who's got time for all that silliness anyway? Remember the standing ovation you got at The

Spot?" she added loud enough for Paulette to hear. That did make Paulette glance over at us curiously.

"You mean *we* got a standing ovation," I reminded Gabriella.

"Anyway," Toby said, glaring at Paulette and her crew as he walked up to Gabriella and me. He popped a mini pizza appetizer in his mouth, and adjusted the sheet over his painting. "What you got under the sheet, Mina?"

"Omigod, my nerves," Gabriella said, fanning herself. "How can you eat?"

"Come on, now," Toby said. "Hold it together. This isn't a big deal — just a friendly exchange of artwork among friends. Plus, the mini pizza and spinach apps are kinda the bomb."

"That's easy for you to say," I snapped. "You've done this before. With her in the room," I said, jabbing my finger in Paulette's direction. "I agree with Gabriella — I think I might faint. What if what I did isn't original enough? You know Ms. Roberts is always giving me a hard time about that."

"Uh-huh, not now. Looks like it's about to go down," Gabriella said. She grabbed me and pulled me into a hug. "Good luck, Mina. You so rock!"

"Thanks, Gabriella," I said, hugging back. "You do, too!"

Ms. Roberts's voice broke up our mutual lovefest.

"Welcome, everyone, to our annual SoHo Children's Art Program," she boomed into the microphone at the front of the room. "Today, we are here to celebrate art and our children's contribution to it. They've been working hard all summer to create their own masterpieces to show off here at our final art show, and we're quite excited to show off their work. At this time, we are going to ask our students to remove their art coverings and remain standing by their paintings so that they can answer any questions the judges and our parents may have. And before the evening is over, we will know which of our talented artists will win the honor of having his or her work appear on our upcoming fall catalog."

My heart tapped to her every word. Gabriella took my hand, Toby took the other, and we wished one another luck. I snuck a look at Paulette, who was standing only two paintings down from mine, her nose stuck so high up in the air that if it were raining, she'd drown. But when I looked at her eyes, she was staring into the spectator section. My eyes followed to where hers were focused. A woman sitting next to a man, who looked exactly like a male version of Paulette, waved at her. Paulette didn't bother waving; she seemed more focused on the man, who was talking on his phone, distracted from everything going on around him. Paulette winced and turned away from the cold scene; when she did, her eyes locked into mine. She looked . . . sad.

And in that very moment, I felt sad, too. Maybe Gabriella had been right. Maybe Paulette felt she had to be cruel in camp, because of the rejection she felt at home.

"Okay, young artists, show us your work!" Ms. Roberts said. The crowd's applause snapped both me and Paulette out of our daze.

There were lots of "oohs" and "ahhs" flowing all through the room as mothers and fathers, sisters and brothers, grandmothers and cousins and aunties and neighbors circulated through the camp art room–turned–gallery, taking in all the work. My parents congratulated me, then disappeared to look at the other work, coming back just in time to witness the judging.

"So, Mina," Ms. Roberts said, walking up with a group of camp counselors who helped us with our art lessons during our in-class sessions. "Tell me about this piece."

"Well, it's, um . . ." I stuttered.

"Take your time," my dad whispered as he rubbed my back. "You can do it."

I looked at him nervously, and then focused back on my artwork. I flashed back to the framed picture of me and my best friends at Auntie's house, and the cowboy lizard Liza sent me and how strong and confident it had made me feel just an hour or so ago. I thought about the sunglasses and T-shirt Samantha had sent me, how it had reminded me of the beach and the place I loved best. Then I looked at my artwork.

On the canvas was me and Samantha and Liza in our bathing suits, lying on our favorite towels. Samantha wore a sun hat, Liza was sipping on a soda in a fancy glass with an umbrella peeking over the rim, and I was right there in between them, my face toward the sun.

My shoulders automatically loosened, and my heart stopped pounding against my chest. I looked Ms. Roberts right in her eyes and started gabbing like she was my best friend.

"Well, I call this one 'Tar Beach,'" I began. "If you know anything about me, you know that my best friends, Samantha and Liza, and I *love* the beach and up until this summer, I thought you needed sand, and, like, the ocean to call a beach a beach, but Gabriella and my auntie and all of her friends taught me that you don't need sand or water to be on a beach. Just the sun. That's me and my friends Samantha and Liza up on my auntie's tar beach, looking up into the sun," I gushed, my words practically running into one another.

"Whoa, do you have any breath left?" my little sister asked as she sipped a bubbly cup of soda. My mother cut her eyes and put her pointer finger to her lips.

"I see that you used all different kinds of objects and paper to add to your painting," Ms. Roberts said. She and the counselors did a collective lean into my picture.

"Yes, I did," I said. My stomach did a somersault waiting for Ms. Roberts to tell me I didn't push enough with my collage. But she didn't say it. She just pulled back and said, "Thank you." And then she and the counselors moved on to Gabriella's project — a lady dancing in a bright, colorful skirt and wide-brimmed hat in the middle of a flower-filled field — without another word.

"Omigosh, I need something to drink," I said, grabbing my sister's cup out of her hands.

"Hey!" she protested.

"Quiet, you two," my mom said. "You're being way too loud for us to be in public."

"The drinks are over there on the table, Mina," my sister huffed.

"Good, go get another one," I said, gulping down her soda. "Make that two."

"Relax, you did great," Auntie Jill said, squeezing my arm. "It really is a great picture."

"I don't know — she's never been a real fan," I said, biting my lip as I watched Ms. Roberts move methodically from one piece of artwork to the next. When she got to Paulette's, she looked way more giddy than she'd been during the entire judging. "See? Ms. Roberts is practically drooling over Paulette's painting. What is that, anyway?" I asked.

Everyone took a collective step back to get a better look at Paulette's picture. It was a picture of the inside of a humongous orange flower with a bee drinking nectar from its insides.

"I like it," my sister said.

I hated to admit it, but I did, too.

Paulette flipped her hair and gave her necklace a little tug. The woman who waved at her earlier patted her shoulder. But the man who looked just like her — her dad — was still on his phone, not really paying attention to what was going on.

Paulette actually looked nervous. Her dad absent-mindedly reached out and offered his hand to Ms. Roberts as she was about to move on, though he still continued to talk in his cell phone. Paulette looked like she wanted to melt into the floor.

Wow, maybe she was human after all.

While Ms. Roberts and the counselors finished looking at the pictures, talking to the campers, and shaking the parents' hands, Gabriella and I took a walk around to check out the competition. Of course, we ended up right in front of Paulette's flower, along with pretty much everybody else in our class. "I love the bumblebee," Stephanie said.

"Yeah, especially the part where it's actually drinking from the flower. It looks so realistic," Mariska added.

"Yeah, definitely the kind of picture Ms. Roberts likes," Stephanie said.

My shoulders dropped. They were all right. There was no way I was going to win against Paulette.

"Your picture's really nice," I told her sincerely.

Paulette looked in my direction; I saw Mariska and Stephanie smirking out of the corner of my eye. Paulette, taking her cue from them, squared her shoulders and said, "Of course it is."

I narrowed my eyes. *Wow — did she really just verbally slap me down after I handed her a compliment on a platter?* I looked at Gabriella and then at Stephanie and Mariska.

"Okay," I said, hesitating at first, and then going with my gut. "You know, Paulette, the proper thing to do when someone pays you a compliment is to say, 'thank you.' That's Etiquette 101."

"Ooh, oh no, she didn't," Stephanie said, folding her arms and looking at Paulette, waiting for her to spew some wisecracking words.

This time, though, Paulette hesitated. And the more she shrank back, the stronger I felt.

"Paulette, you've been mean to me from the moment I walked through the door, even though I never gave you a reason to be anything but a friend. I don't feel bad about it, though, because I didn't do anything wrong. I just feel sorry for you. If the only way you can feel good about yourself or your situation is to put someone else down, then do it. But do me a favor and leave me out of it."

Paulette looked dumbstruck.

"Hello," said the lady who'd been waving at Paulette, as she walked up with a cup of lemonade. She handed it to Paulette. "Who's your friend?" she asked.

Paulette didn't say anything, and refused the drink.

"Well," said the woman, a tall, well-dressed blond with sad hazel eyes. "I'm Paulette's mom."

"Actually, she's my stepmom," Paulette corrected forcefully.

Paulette's father, who'd been totally out of the loop and seemingly not listening to the conversation while he jabbered on the phone, certainly heard his daughter.

"Paulette!" he yelled, cupping his hand over the mouthpiece of his phone. "Your tone. Correct it," he said.

"Sorry, Daddy," Paulette practically wimpered.

We all got really quiet, unsure of what to say next. Truthfully, I felt sorry for Paulette. Clearly, she had home issues that she really didn't need everyone in camp to witness.

"Um, Paulette," I finally said in hopes of easing the tension. "I just wanted to tell you that your picture is really amazing, and I think both of us are pretty good artists. Different, but definitely talented. Good luck with the contest."

And with that, I walked off. This time with a smile on my face.

Just then, Toby, who'd spent the last ten minutes making lame attempts to listen in on the counselor deliberations while he swallowed practically a whole tray of those mini pizza thingies, came back over to give us news about what he heard. "I got nothing," he said, shaking his head. "Nothing!"

"Oh my goodness, Toby, will you go sit down somewhere?" Gabriella said. "You're making my nerves bad."

"Okay, everyone," Ms. Roberts said into the mike, startling us all. "I need some quiet, everyone. We are ready to announce the winner."

The whole room grew dramatically quiet. Gabriella grabbed my hand. I glanced at Paulette; she glanced back and gave me a half smile.

"And the winner of this year's SoHo Children's Art Program is," Ms. Roberts said, pausing for effect. Paulette leaned in closer. We all did. "Mina Chestnut!"

Now, I wasn't quite sure what she said, because I really wasn't hearing anything; I just saw Gabriella jumping up and down like a lunatic, and my little sister smiling, and my mom and dad and auntie over in the section where the chairs were, raising their arms in the air and yelling. Everyone seemed to be moving in slow motion. The first voice I really heard was Paulette's. "Mina," she said, “you have to go up front now. Congratulations. You totally deserve it.”

I felt her hand on the small of my back; it was pushing me forward. I turned and looked at Paulette; she seemed genuine. And for this, I was grateful. I knew I’d never be best friends with Paulette, but it was nice that we were going to leave on a pretty good note.

“Mina, come on up,” Ms. Roberts said. I gave one last look to Paulette, hugged Gabriella, and made my way toward Ms. Roberts. My mouth was open so wide a fly could have easily dive-bombed into it and made a home in my throat. The room continued applauding.

“Mina’s fantastic collage was chosen for its spirit and its originality. It is clear that she took a chance in her art — something we’d been encouraging her to do the entire summer. Her mixed-media collage, titled ‘Tar Beach,’ shows that she stretched beyond her boundaries, and not only incorporated the lessons she learned here in the classroom, but the lessons she learned while being a visitor to our great city. We present to you, Mina Chestnut and her fabulous piece, ‘Tar Beach’!”

One of the counselors, George, brought

it to the front of the room and held it up next to me.

"As a reward for her hard work, Mina's 'Tar Beach' will be featured on the fall catalog of the SoHo Children's Art Program, a magazine that goes out to literally thousands of people, showing them all of the wonderful programming we have here for children of all backgrounds who are lovers of art. Congratulations again, Mina!"

"Thank you," was all I could think to say as I looked out over the crowd and saw the faces of the people I love. "Thank you!"

I looked down at my lucky Converses and searched for Samantha and Liza's signatures. I wished they were there to see it — my best friends.

But it was going to be one great story to tell them when we finally did see one another again.

And that wouldn't be too long from now.

Not too long at all.

I flipped to a clean sheet of paper, pulled out a pencil, then sat back and waited for the show. Just a couple more turns and then my dad would pull the car onto the Brooklyn Bridge and there she'd be — the Statue of Liberty. This time, though, I had my oil pastels — every color in the rainbow.

And the moment I saw her, I was going to paint her in loud, bold colors. Maybe some purple. And a rainbow of buildings behind her. And star sparkles shooting from her eternal flame. Yeah, that would work.

Something bold.

Something new.

Something like the new me.

It was amazing how much I'd learned over the past weeks: how to make new friends, even as I held on to the memory of my old ones; how to speak up for myself, even when I was afraid; how to appreciate who I am, even when who I am didn't fall in line with what others around me were. I even learned to like tofu. Well, kinda.

I looked out the window again, and there she was: Lady Liberty.

"You think maybe I could have a piece of paper, Mina?" my sister asked. "And a hot-pink crayon? I think I want to draw the statue, too."

"Sure," I said, handing my sister a piece of paper and smiling at her. "I bet you she'll look really pretty in pink."

Check out the other books in the Candy Apple Summer Trilogy!

Enjoy this special sneak peek at

Wish You Were Here, Liza

by Robin Wasserman

Location: Cheap-O Car Rental, Chicago, IL
Population: 2.8 million
Miles Driven: 0
Days of Torment: 1 (felt like 100)

There were a few problems with the Great Gold Family Summer Vacation. For one thing, there was nothing great about it. For another, it wasn't *just* the Gold family.

When I was little, we went on a lot of trips with my parents' friends, the Kaplan-Novaks and the

Schwebers. And now that family vacation was back, the Kaplan-Novaks and the Schwebers were back, too. And so were their kids.

We met them at the car rental place by the airport. While my parents filled out forms, I grabbed a paper cup of lukewarm water and ducked outside.

"Isn't this awesome?" Dillie Kaplan-Novak said to me right away.

I looked around. There were junky cars, tired tourists, heat waves rising from the black cement — but definitely no awesomeness. "Um, what?"

"This!" Dillie rocked back and forth on the balls of her feet. "I've been so psyched for this trip. I can't believe we get to go away for the *whole* summer. It'll be just like the old days."

"Right. Totally." I was starting to get that feeling in my stomach. Like last summer at the amusement park when I'd eaten one too many bags of cotton candy.

You never know, Mina had told me at our "See Ya Soon" party. (Because best friends never say "good-bye.") *Maybe you'll like them.*

Yeah, Sam had added. *You might decide to trade us in for new best friends.*

You've got nothing *to worry about,* I thought, missing them already.

Enjoy this special sneak peek at

by Lara Bergen

My mom rolled down the windows, and that unmistakable beachy smell filled the car: salt, sand, and coconut oil. I took a deep breath. This beach road was a lot different than the ones in New Jersey. Where were all the T-shirt shops and ice-cream stands? Where was the amusement park? All this place had were beach houses, as far as I could see.

"So, uh, where's the boardwalk?" I finally asked my mother.

"Oh, I don't think there is one, honey," she said.

"No boardwalk? So what do kids *do* here?" I asked her.

"Well . . ." She shrugged. "I guess they go to the beach."

Every day? For eight weeks?

Finally, we turned off the main road. Before I knew it, we were driving toward a big house with a sign on the front that said ISLE BE BACK.

"Is that it?" I asked my mother. "Wow, it's pretty cool! That roof deck looks like fun. And it has a pool! And a tennis court, too?" I almost hated to admit it, but this place was going to be awesome!

"Huh?" my mom said absentmindedly. "Tennis court? Pool? Oh no, hon. That's not it." She laughed. Then she drove right by the house and pointed to another one behind it. "There you go. The Drift Inn. That's us." She turned off the car's engine.

I'd seen some big houses, but this thing was out of control. Way bigger than the other house I'd been looking at. So big that there wasn't even *room* for a tennis court or pool around it. I'd assumed it was some kind of old hotel or school or something.

And by "old," I mean . . . a *total* mess.

Accidentally Fabulous

Accidentally Famous

Accidentally Fooled

Accidentally Friends

How to Be a Girly Girl in Just Ten Days

Miss Popularity

Miss Popularity Goes Camping

Making Waves

Juicy Gossip

Life, Starring Me!

Callie for President

Totally Crushed

Wish You Were Here, Liza

See You Soon, Samantha

Miss You, Mina

Winner Takes All